Richard Hooker Wilmer, Whitemarsh Benjamin Seabrook

Saved by a Woman

The Hidden Romance

Richard Hooker Wilmer, Whitemarsh Benjamin Seabrook

Saved by a Woman
The Hidden Romance

ISBN/EAN: 9783337346980

Printed in Europe, USA, Canada, Australia, Japan

Cover: Foto ©Andreas Hilbeck / pixelio.de

More available books at **www.hansebooks.com**

SAVED BY A WOMAN;

OR,

THE HIDDEN ROMANCE.

A STORY OF THE LATE WAR.

By STROBHART.

ATLANTA, GA.:

JAS. P. HARRISON & CO., PRINTERS AND BINDERS.

1884.

Dedication.

FIRST,

TO MY GENTLE, AND AFFECTIONATE MOTHER;

AND NEXT,

TO MY BRETHREN OF THE TELEGRAPHIC PROFESSION,

THIS BOOK IS AFFECTIONATELY AND

FRATERNALLY DEDICATED.

—AUTHOR.

AUGUSTA, GA.,

January 4th, 1884.

PREFACE.

THE narrative which follows, is based upon a series of truthful adventures. The hero of the work, actually "lives, moves and has his being." He tells his own unpolished story plainly, as a soldier, and not as a writer, and modestly, as merely a man, and not as a hero. If there have been added any embellishments they do not materially conflict with the truthful telling of the tale; if there has been introduced anything unreal, it has only been so much as was deemed requisite to supply the "missing links" in the broken chain of truthful incidents. So much is said on purpose to show that the writer's privileges have been greatly restricted. To have introduced his hero into scenes and incidents wholly imaginary, would have been, to say the least, impertinent; while to have followed unswervingly the veracious channel of his adventures, would have been to endanger the interest of the tale. For these reasons, therefore, the writer's task has not been an easy one; nor is it probable, that he has succeeded in wholly obliterating every damaging evidence of a restrained imagination. * * * * * Even under auspices, the most favorable, a thousand doubts might well assail an unknown "scribe," who is preparing to thrust himself into public notice; but for the reasons above enumerated, these misgivings are greatly multiplied.

The story, however, in the judgment of the writer, possesses intrinsically much which is interesting; and if in this opinion he succeeds in inducing the public to concur, he will have accomplished his object, and obtained his reward.

"AUTHOR."

SAVED BY A WOMAN.

CHAPTER I.

*   *   *   *   *   *   *

It was in the spring of '61 that I voluntered my
services to "Dixie." The ominous war-clouds, which
had for months, even for years, hung brooding over
our peaceful land, had burst at last upon it, with
mighty and appalling thunder. The smoke of battle
had hung like a pall, over Sumter, and death had
already begun its abundant harvest in the east. Even
at this early stage of the strife, the cry for volunteers
resounded through the land, to find a responsive echo
in every patriotic heart. Men of low degree and
high, rich men and poor, old men and beardless
youths, were hurrying to the front from all points of
the compass; some to reap honors and fame, others
to be brought back maimed for life, and many, alas,
how many, never to return. It was at this time, (in
the spring of '61, as I have said), that I too should-
ered my knapsack and turning my back upon a well
loved home, started to join the 16th Tennessee regiment. How full of life, and hope, was I, on that bright
spring morning as I mounted my impatient steed and
rode away, and how well, even now, do I recall the
sorrowful scenes at parting. The tears and prayers
of an affectionate mother, the blessings and counsels
of an aged father, all these I see, and feel, as plainly

now as then. But I must not linger o'er them. With the mournful cadence of the oft-repeated "Good-bye" still ringing in my ears, and in my heart too, for that matter, I reined in my horse upon a hillock hard-by and took my "last lingering look" at the beloved home which I was deserting, perhaps forever. I shall never forget the picture which then I beheld. Leaning upon the garden fence, his head bowed upon his swelling breast and his gray locks waving in the early morning breeze, feebly stood my father. Behind him in the doorway was my dear mother, alternately waving her handkerchief to me and wiping her eyes with it, and even at that distance, I imagined I could hear her last prayerful words following me, in broken utterance, "God bless you, my boy, and bring you safely back to mother." I felt a choking sensation in my throat as I looked, and before I knew it, burning tears were coursing down my cheeks. I took off my military cap, raised it in a last salute, and putting spurs to my horse, dashed away. This was my last farewell to my mother. I never saw her more; but the blessing of her last words has warmed my heart full many a time since then. Alas! that we should receive so lightly these blessings while we hear them uttered, and that it should require the stamp—even of death—to give them a right impression upon our hearts.

But there is little room for gloomy reflection in the breast of a youth just twenty-one years of age, and before I had completed the half of my journey to camp, my hopes were as high and my spirits as buoyant as ever. I must pass rapidly over; nay, I must not even glance at the events of the first eighteen months of my military service. At the end of that time I was still only a private, but I was beginning to find favor with my officers, and I had then every reasonable hope of soon taking an upward step in rank. I had made, and alas, I had lost many friends during that period, and now I was to lose the dearest friend of all—my mother. The news of her death came upon me with crushing force. For a while it stunned me, and I went the round of my daily duties like one in a dream. "Troubles never come singly," they say, and with me so it proved, for hard upon the news of this great affliction, I was taken suddenly ill, and lay for weeks with scarce a span 'twixt me and death. When I at last arose I was more ghost than man. I was offered a furlough without the trouble of asking for it, but this I refused. I could not go home, now that there was no longer a mother to welcome me there, and I asked to be assigned to post duty until my health should improve. Accordingly I was sent as steward to the hospital at Atlanta, and here, under the able treatment of Dr. Eave, the physician in charge, I rapidly regained my health and was soon pronounced sufficiently well to rejoin my regiment. A circumstance occurred, however, which rendered this impossible, and which, as will soon be seen, changed my entire future. I had conceived the plan of visiting my afflicted father while on my way to the front, but as there were many difficulties to be overcome, before this could be accomplished, I determined to consult with Dr. Eave as to the plausibility of the project. Accordingly I sought him out, in his private office, and after laying before him my wishes and doubts I asked what he thought of the scheme.

"Where do you live?" asked the doctor after a moments reflection.

"In McMinnville, Tennessee, sir," said I.

"What," said he, jumping from his seat excitedly.

"Why, my dear fellow, you are the very man I am looking for."

"If I can render you a service doctor,"—

"You can sir, you can, said he, interrupting me," a most valuable service, if you will; but let me explain. "I am sadly in need of a case of surgical instruments here, and they cannot be found." "There is'nt such a thing in the city of Atlanta, and the the North, you know, is blockaded." "Now, there is but one way out of the difficulty, and that is to send or go for my own." Do you follow me.

"You wish me to get them for you?"

"Exactly sir; you have hit it."

"And where do you live, may I ask?"

"Where do I live? Why my dear sir," said the doctor, we are neighbors. My home and those instruments are less than twenty miles from your father's house in McMinnville."

It is scarcely necessary to say, that I eagerly accepted this opportunity of combining duty with pleasure, and it took me but a short time to receive my directions, get my "leave" signed and start, upon the most eventful journey of my life.

Two days later I arrived in Chattanooga; my first act upon reaching here, being to seek out General Ledbetter, then in command of the city, state my business and procure a passport through the lines. Besides giving me the passport and wishing me a kind "God-speed," the General volunteered the advice that I should make the remainder of my journey in citizen's dress, and, accordingly, I lost no time in making the necessary purchases. My uniform and papers, except my pass, I left with a chance friend for safe keeping; and he kept them safely enough, for I have never seen uniform, papers or friend since.

CHAPTER II.

I am now about to relate an occurrence which made but little impression upon me at the time of its happening, but which I had abundant and most startling reasons for remembering more than once afterwards.

On the night of my arrival in Chattanooga, after having arranged everything for my journey as before stated, I sauntered into the hotel barber shop, intending to have my then very heavy moustache taken off, with the view of helping my disguise, for inasmuch as I was traveling in a country in which I was well known I did not deem the precaution superfluous. I found the shop crowded, and not wishing to spend an hour amid tobacco smoke and profanity, I left directions for a barber to come to me, and betook myself to my room. I had not long to wait. A cautious knock at my room door announced the arrival of the barber, and a moment later a dried up little man with a very oily head and a tongue to correspond, bowed himself into the room. His peculiar accent at once proclaimed him a Frenchman.

"If Monsieur" be ready he would have "ze honeur." "Monsieur" had un grande, vat you call him—moustach-cha. He hoped "Monsieur" did not intend to part "vid dat."

I was not in the humor to be flattered, and setting his scruples at rest, I abruptly bade him proceed with his task. During the few moments of preparation which followed the Frenchman talked incessantly asking question after question, and never once waiting for a reply, rattled on in a manner that quite confused me. He was approaching me, at length, scissors in hand, and I was in the act of throwing back my head in the proper position for shaving, when he suddenly stopped and began to gaze in my direction, with such horror stealing over his countenance as I had never seen upon human face before. Involuntarily I started and looked behind me, expecting to see I know not what, but there was nothing but empty space between me and the wall.

"What's the matter, my man?" I asked; "you look as if you had seen a ghost!"

"Ghost! Aye, ghost!" said the Frenchman in a half whisper; "mon Dieu, Monsieur, it was a ghost."

The Frenchman's face by this time was as white as the sheet which I had pinned around my neck, and, trembling in every limb, he sunk into a convenient chair, where he sat fairly gasping for breath. I did my utmost to laugh away the poor fellow's fears, but all in vain. There was no reasoning with him, and he swore persistently that he had seen the white-robed form of a woman standing against the wall just behind me, and that it vanished as quick as he saw it. Finding, at length, that I could not reason him out of his evident belief, I became a little vexed at what I termed his stupidity, and bade him shave me at once or begone; but this he declared he could not do. He must positively compose himself, he said, before he could attempt so delicate an operation, and he hoped Monsieur would pardon him. This announcement irritated me beyond measure, and I am afraid I slammed the door upon the retreating Frenchman before he had fairly passed through it. Thus ended my hope of being shaved before I commenced my journey.

The next morning was bright and clear. The sun

was just gilding the top of "Lookout Mountain" as, seated beside several others, in a common plantation wagon, I passed out of Chattancoga and anon reached the first line of pickets. Here we showed our passes and proceeded to the second and last picket line ; where again we produced our passports, and, after they had been examined, destroyed them. Thus far I had paid little attention to my companions, but now, being on dangerous ground, we became as by mutual consent, quite sociable. What power is there half so equalizing in its effect, as the shadow of a common danger ?

To judge from outward appearances, we were a party of peaceable civilians, who knew nothing of the war, and cared as little about it ; for certain it is that we seldom spoke of it. The weather, the scenery around us and the products of the country through which we were passing, were the subjects which engrossed our conversation, and, at the end of a dozen miles of travel, we knew as little of each other as when we started.

Owing to the fact that our route lay directly across the mountains, our progress was slow and laborious, and at noon we had only compassed about fourteen miles of our journey. We were now upon the extreme top of the range, and had halted to give our horses a moment to "wind," when we were rather startled by the abrupt appearance of a man, who stood before us so suddenly as to create the delusion that he had dropped from the clouds, while in reality, he had only stepped from behind a tree. He was dressed as a farmer, and carried a shot gun upon his shoulder.

"Mornin," said he, as with a grin, he acknowledged our looks of surprise.

" Why, good morning, sir ; said the driver, at once assuming the roll of spokesman.

"Dy'e know," said the stranger, pointing over his shoulder, "that thar's lots on em right afore you?"

"Lot's o' what?" asked the driver.

"Yanks," said the stranger;" Yanks, and as sure's you live you're waltzin into a hornet's nest.

"Have you seen them?" I asked, becoming myself interested.

"I have," said he stepping a few paces nearer to us; "and now that I am satisfied, gentlemen, that you are all Confederates, I no longer hesitate in telling you that I am not what I seem."

"A scout," said I.

"Exactly sir; one of Morgan's."

This announcement had the double effect of greatly surprising us, and of increasing our interest in the stranger, and we at once began to ply him with questions concerning the proximity of the enemy, their force, and so forth.

"It is true," said he. "There is a full regiment of Blue-coats, marching toward Chattanooga, and they must pass this spot in less than two hours. It is not to your liking, I dare assert, but your only course is to turn back, and the quicker you do it the better."

"And you," said I, "what will become of you?"

"Oh!" said he, smiling, "I have other fish to fry."

The scout had spoken truly. We did not fancy a retreat; nevertheless, it was plainly the one course left open to us. Thanking him therefore for his timely warning, and bidding him good-day, we were soon beating a hasty retreat, and at sunset, we had retraced our steps to within three miles of the outer picket-post of the city. Here we stopped at a farm-house to water our horses, and were both surprised and alarmed to learn from the farmer that there was a considerable force of the enemy between us and the city, putting us literally between two fires. A hasty consultation was held, and we were not long in deciding upon a course of action. This, in a few words, was to journey across the country to a Mr. Poe's, a well-known Southern man, distant about twelve miles from where we then were, and arriving there to remain until it should be deemed prudent for us to continue our journey. Having received directions from the farmer we therefore sat out at once, and a little before midnight we were safely within sight of Poe's farm. But here another surprise awaited us. Within the spacious enclosure around the farmer's cottage, sparkled no less than a dozen camp-fires, and not wishing to proceed blindfolded into what might prove a camp of the enemy, we halted to reconnoitre. Volunteering my services, I went cautiously forward on foot. All seemed peaceful and quiet as I approached. Not a sound broke the stillness of the night, save now and then the "cracking" of the dying camp-fire; the occasional "stamp" of a horse's foot upon the earth, or the grinding of his teeth together, as he munched the last of his supper, and I had reached to within a few yards of the enclosure, and still no sign of human life presented itself; but here, after intently looking about me, in every direction, I at length made out the indistinct outlines of a human form leaning against a tree near to one of the fires. The light was too indistinct, however, for me to decide the question as to whether he was "Union" or "Confederate," and until this question was decided I dared not show myself. There was nothing for it, therefore, but to wait where I was, and trust to chance for the rest. Having made up my mind to this I walked quite up to the fence, and was preparing to sit down and make myself as comfortable as possible, when I felt a heavy hand grasp my shoulder, and ere I could think of resistance, the cold muzzle of a revolver was pressed against my temple.

"Better to keep quiet, I guess," said a low voice in my ear," wouldn't like to make a sifter o' your brain-house—understand."

"I understand quite well. You have all the advantage , said I. What do you want with me?"

"Don't know as I want you at all," said the man, who now lowered his weapon, and stood in front of me— "Depends entirely upon the color o' your liver."

"Well, really my friend," said I—"Considering the fact that I have never had the opportunity of discovering in what particulars my individual liver"—

"Balderdash," said the man. "What's your sentiments, gray or blue? Out with it."

"I am a Confederate."

"Can you prove it?"

"Impossible—I have destroyed all proof of my identity."

"Come, no nonsense," said he ;" show your papers; but hold, it is not necessary now that I look at you."
"I met you to-day."

I soon discovered that this was true. The scout whom we had met in the morning, and the man before me was one and the same person.

"How in the name of wonder, are you here?" said I, jumping to my feet; for his heavy hand had precipitated me into a sitting posture.

"Oh!" said he. "I am a fast walker ; but what are *you* doing here?"

"Sit down and you shall hear—but what a walker you must be."

"Behold!" said he, with a low chuckle as he stretched a huge limb before me. "See the length,

the shape, the thickness, and no longer wonder;"—
but proceed with your story.

We now sat down, and began to exchange confidence. After relating to him the circumstances
which had led to our second meeting, he proceeded
to give me all the information I desired. By a short
cut through the woods he had arrived at Poe's about
dark, and found there stragglers from all directions
to the number of about thirty. These were all presumably Confederates, but as there could be no certainty upon this head, every man was shy of his
neighbor. Poe himself did not know the true sentiments of half his guests. Scarcely his guests either,
inasmuch as his abundant hospitality was forced upon him. He (Poe) was about to abandon his place.
He would leave next morning with his stock and
whatever valuables he could carry, for some safe retreat in the mountains, and the scout advised us to
join his party. There were animals enough he said
for all to ride, and we would thus be helping Poe
and forwarding our own ends at the same time. In
the scouts opinion this was the wisest, if not the only
course we could safely pursue. After a little further
conversation I parted with him, who was about leaving for parts only known to himself, and hastening
back to my companions proceeded to lay before them
what I had learned together with the plans suggested.

There was little need for a pilot in plain sailing
like this, and with one accord we determined to cast
our lot with that of Mr. Poe. In less than an hour
later, therefore, we had taken quiet possession of that
gentleman's barnyard, and had made ourselves as comfortable for the night as our surroundings permitted.

2

CHAPTER III.

"After a few hours of refreshing slumber I awoke
to find it already daylight. Men in every character
of dress were hurrying to and fro, some saddling their
animals, some stowing away the remnants of their
breakfast, some filling their canteens at the well, and
o'hers strapping on their weapons, or packing their
luggage. Everything betokened a hasty departure.
At a little distance away, in an open pasture, grazed
a herd of about two hundred cattle, while in the yard
in which we were, young mules, sheep, swine, goats and
every species of fowl were huddled together in strange
confusion. I shall never forget the mournful melody
of their mingled voices. The 'bellowing' of the cows,
the bleating of the sheep, the more indistinct 'grunt'
of the hogs, and the occasional shrill crow of a cock,
or cackle of a hen, combined to make sad, though—
not unpleasant music. But the stir and bustle of
preparation added a harsh accompaniment and robbed
the effect of its peaceful suggestion. Who that lived
in those dark days cannot recall some scene similar
to this? The desertion of a long loved home, the
rude breaking asunder of all those ties and associa-
tions, which have hitherto combined to make up so
much of our happiness. At such moments we not
only feel an uncertain dread of what the future may
hold for us, but our hearts are filled with a tender
concern, wholly free from vulgar or mercenary considerations, for 'the dear old place' which we are
leaving without a protector. A tender concern?
Aye, truly this, for each familiar object that we look

upon reveals at this parting moment some new feature
to admire, if not an actual beauty, never before remarked. Trifles which had no value yesterday, are
almost treasures to-day; and the meanest gewgaw
which we yesterday spurned, we are strangely careful
of to-day. Alas, that so many should have known
the feeling, and that in so many instances their dark-
est forebodings should have been re lized to the full.
Alas, again that the devastating hand of war should
so often o'er reach ourselves and invade the sacred
precincts of our homes. But to my story.

Without waiting to see that my companions were
stirring, I left the wagon in which we had all slept,
and hastened away to find our host; my object being
to obtain his consent to our joining his party and to
borrow some animals for our use. I found him with
little trouble—an open-faced, genial man of about
sixty—and he readily gave his consent to all I asked.
We could have as many mules as we desired he said,
and he would be delighted to have our company.
With this report I returned to my companions, where
I found a hastily prepared breakfast awaiting me, of
which I heartily partook, and this duty performed we
were ready for the road. Mounting upon my young
and fractious mule, I was one of the last to leave the
enclosure. Our host had lingered behind to give
some last directions to a negro, the only servant he
was leaving; and, as the animal I bestrode suddenly
concluded to go no further, coax and spur him as I
would, I made a virtue of necessity and patiently
awaited the coming of the farmer. It was now broad
daylight. The sun just kissed the tops of the tall
pines and touched a hillock here and there, as if to
dry up the tears the night had shed, and bid "the
hills rejoice," because it had come again. Green

pastures stretched away on every hand from which, now and then a field lark rose high in air, uttering its melodious offering to the morning.

Just rising a gentle incline to my left, was the cavalcade, which had preceeded me; the "smack" of the long lash, the peculiar "hia," "hia," of the drivers and the "tramp" and bellowing of the cattle, becoming momentarily less distinct; and behind me, nestling peacefully among venerable oaks and cedars, stood the deserted home of the farmer. At the gate through which I had just passed, the latter already mounted, was in the act of bidding farewell to his trusted slave, when, looking toward the train, I noticed with surprise, that instead of taking the proffered hand of his master, the negro suddenly began to gesticulate excitedly, and to point in the direction of the house. In another moment the negro had disappeared as if by magic, and the master was galloping at full speed straight toward me. With some anxiety I waited his coming, to learn the meaning of his hurried flight, but long before he reached me, the cause became but too apparent. The Yankees were upon us. Charging through the yard, having approached unseen from behind the house, came on in hot pursuit à full company of blue-coated cavalry. Mr. Poe swept by me like the wind, calling to me to follow, and my hitherto refractory animal, catching something of the spirit of the moment, answered the spur right bravely, and dashed after him. For a few moments we held our own, and the hope of escape beat high in my heart. The cool air of the morning and the lively pace at which I was going, together with the excitement of the moment, produced in me a kind of intoxication, intensely pleasurable; but the pleasure was short-lived. Mr. Poe was distancing me, and my animal losing the companionship of the farmer's noble charger began to lag; and, alas! no persuasion on my part, whether gentle or the reverse, could induce him to save me from capture. I now realized this painful truth, and yet I did not cease my struggles until my pursuer's were actually abreast of me, and I heard the command to surrender, accompanied by the ominous "click" of several revolvers. To struggle unarmed against such odds would have been madness, and ere I had fully realized the unpleasant fact, I was a prisoner.

CHAPTER IV.

In less time than it takes me to tell it, I was left in the custody of two men, and the troops had swept by us, hard upon the heels of Mr. Poe.

"Got'cher silf in a nice kittle o' fish," said one of my captors. "Got any bull pups about 'cher?"

"I am not armed, if that is what you mean," I answered.

"Oh! You are not? P'rap's you have some "dust," then? No! Nor a "ticker" neither?"

"What I have is my own," I said "and if you dare rob me, I shall report it to your officers at the first opportunity."

"O'ho, that's the tune is, it? Well, I reckon, I don't want'cher greasy Confed. "shin plasters," nor yer brass turnip, neither; so you need not fire off yer lip, "Johnnie Reb." We don't like it."

By this time I had dismounted, and was being marched back toward the farm house; upon reaching which I was surprised to find no less than fifty

prisoners surrounded by a small guard. I was unceremoniously shoved in among these, and left to
mingle with them as I pleased ; and I began at once
to look about me wondering if among all these unfortunates there might not be found at least one face
with whom I was familiar. There were men of every
age, from the lad of sixteen to the old man of sixty
years or more. There was also every species of dress
among them ; the common home-spun of the farmer ;
the more fastidious dress of "the man from town ;"
the rags of the pauper, and in a few instances
the full Confederate uniform, were all to be seen.
But a single common feature pervaded the company, and this consisted in the anxious look which
marked every countenance. I was just beginning
to despair of finding any among them whom I knew,
when I noticed something of a commotion among the
guard, and I soon perceived that another prisoner
was being brought in. Prompted by a natural curiosity, I looked toward the latter and, at a single glance,
I knew him as the scout, who had twice befriended us
on the day before. Although I should rather have
felt sorrow at his misfortune, I confess to a selfish
pleasure at seeing him, and I hastened forward to
offer my condolence. Can I say *condolence*, after the
confession I have made ?

"My dear fellow," I began, but I ceased abruptly,
to wonder at the meaningless stare which I encoun-
tered.

"Hist," he said in a low voice. "Be careful you
o not know me *here*."

"Excuse me," said I aloud ; at once catching his
meaning. "I took you for some one else." I was
turning away when he touched me on the shoulder
and continued, "I see there is no one noticing us. *I*

am here from choice. I will escape at the proper moment, but I must not be known as Morgan's scout. The distinction between "scout" and "spy," is but subtile at best, and besides, Morgan's very name is enough to hang me. Do you understand?"

"Perfectly," "but I cannot help wondering at your temerity. How on earth are you to escape?"

"I don't know *how*," said he; "but I am sure I *will* escape." He drew himself proudly up and continued, "I was educated, sir, by John Morgan."

"Good luck to you," I said, adding to myself—"I do not wonder at Morgan's brilliant career, if all his men are like you."

"Many better," said he; his keen ear having caught my soliloquy. "Many better and few not as good. Morgan's men are for the most part educated scouts. I do not speak of all whom he has commanded, but of those whom he always chooses for his sudden raids. There is not one among them but would dare as much as this. Pshaw! This is nothing.

"May I ask your name, sir," said I; becoming much interested in the man.

"Certainly," he replied. "My name is McPherson, Frank McPherson, but better known since the war commenced," added he with a chuckle, as "Slippery Frank." "I hail from near Atlanta, in Georgia." I have been captured and have escaped five times since I joined the army; hence my nickname of "Slippery." I have; and now stranger, y'er curiosity hes took you es fer es i'll foller, so just you git."

I needed not the cunning wink he gave me to understand his sudden change of manner, for just then an officer approached us. Producing a memorandum book and pencil the latter asked us our names, places of residence, etc., displaying an interest in our replies, which would have been quite flattering, under other circumstances. For my part, I gave him my full name, my regiment, and even the letter of my company, for at that moment I could think of no reason for concealing anything of my true character. Having given my answers, I was now all curiosity to hear what those of McPherson would be, nor was I long in finding out.

Before the officer had well reached him, the scout commenced his voluntary information thus: "My name's Speers—Jim Speers—lives in Georgy—farms—travelling to Shelbyville to see some relations; got tuck, and thar's the end of it;" and with this, he stuck both hands into his trowsers' pockets and sauntered away.

The officer smiled while he made a note of this information, but said nothing. Not long after this the troop of cavalry appeared in the distance; and shortly thereafter they rode up, bringing with them about twenty prisoners. Very few, if any, of those, who left the farm in the morning, had escaped. I recognized among the unfortunates all of my late companions, except the driver, whom I learned afterwards, had escaped by hiding in the stable. After lounging about for a half hour to "blow" their horses, during which time Mr. Poe's house was "gone through" from top to bottom, we were formed by twos, and with a strong guard on each side of us, marched off toward the enemy's lines in front of Chattanooga.

Before we reached them, however, an incident occurred, which, as it forms an important link in the chain of my story, must be told in detail; and, therefore, I beg leave to reserve it for another chapter.

CHAPTER V.

"It was high noon when we took the road, attended only by a portion of our captors; the remainder having preceded us by about an hour; driving the farmer's stock toward their lines.

The day was intensely hot. The sun hung in an unclouded sky, and his fiery rays beat full upon us, with suffocating effect. The road, for the most part, was deep in sand, burning particles of which filled our shoes, causing us acute pain, which increased at every step; and to add to our discomfort we were hurried along at a pace little less than a run in order to keep up with the horses of our escort. Taking into consideration the gloomy thoughts which necessarily filled us, our condition was as miserable as could well be.

I could but pity the old and feeble of our party, many of whom, heartsick and already weary, dragged themselves along with an effort painful to behold. There was one old man among the latter who particularly engaged my deepest sympathies. He could scarcely have been less than seventy years of age. His hair and beard were silvery white; his head shook with the palsy of age, and his limbs trembled and tottered at every step. Why was he made a prisoner? Because, on the night before, he had fired upon a body of federals, who were driving away his cattle, and otherwise depredating upon his place. Because he had defended his substance, which in his old age was life itself to him.

He was walking just in front of me; walking did

I say ?—rather dragging his limbs along, while he
supported his body between a stick, and the generously offered arm of a younger man at his side. Now
in consequence of this, the progress of these two was
slower than of the rest of the line, at which delay
the guards became greatly incensed. Curses and
abuses were rained upon us, and threats became
numerous ; but they availed nothing, for the old
man's scanty store of strength was fast failing him,
and every new effort but exhausted it the more. At
length, after a perfect torrent of abuse, and a savage
shove from one of the guard, the aged prisoner stood
still and turning to the nearest officer, a sergeant, said
meekly and feebly : "Sir, if you wish me to go
further you must carry me—were death, the penalty
of halting, I could walk no more."

"See here," said the irate sergeant with an oath,
"you were not too old, nor too feeble, to handle a
shot-gun last night, and by G—d you are not too old
nor too feeble to walk to day"—then springing from
his horse, he drew his sword from the scabbard and
placing the point against the old man's breast ordered
him to march.

"I cannot ; I cannot," he said—"take my life if
you will, but I cannot."

There was murder in the man's eyes. He had
already tightened his grip upon his sword and was in
the act of giving the cowardly thrust, when being
unable longer to restrain myself I leapt upon him like
a panther and felled him to my feet with a single
blow.

"For shame," I cried, "you cowardly cur—you
shall not harm those gray hairs while I live " If ever
there was a countenance to which the phrase "demon-
like" might apply, I saw it at that moment. There

was a smile upon his face that might have frozen my blood, were I less heated with passion ; and his dark eyes emitted flashes of terrible purpose, as he deliberately gained his feet and brushed the sand from his clothes.

Not once did he take his eyes from mine, and I, angry and defiant, met his gaze unflinchingly. For one brief instant did we eye each other thus ; then his right arm was raised slowly towards me, and when it gained the level of my eyes I saw that the hand held a cocked revolver. The weapon was scarce two feet from my face. I watched, with a kind of fascination I could not master, the index finger as it slowly left the guard and reached the trigger.

My heart raised itself in silent supplication, and had I died then my last breath would have gone out in prayer. The finger pressed the trigger, the flash blinded me, the report deafened me, but the ball did me no harm, although, alas ! it found a victim. The innocent cause of all this trouble was standing just behind me, and he it was who received the angry bullet full in his forehead and e'er I could turn my head to look upon him he had sunk to the earth a corpse. This tragic incident consumed in its acting much less time than it takes me to tell it. Officers hurried to scene, attracted thither ; first by the halt in the procession and afterward by the report of the pistol.

From many conflicting reports concerning the affair he in command at last caught the drift of its true character, and at once ordered the murderer to be bound and treated as a prisoner.

As to myself he said, "Considering the end, I am sorry you interfered in this business, but I nevertheless commend your motive."

"I could not have foreseen the issue sir," said I, and I meant to jeopardize no one's life but my own."

The officer now gave some orders which I could not overhear, and two of the escorts dismounting removed the lifeless body to one side of the road and the procession was again put in motion, leaving behind the two soldiers keeping guard over their dead prisoner. I marched along after this with many conflicting emotions struggling within me for the mastery. I burned with indignation, because that so little respect had been shown in the first instance for one of the victims of age and infirmity, and that he should have been ruthlessly compelled to encounter hardships which might have taxed the hardihood of many a younger man. And while I deeply deplored the tragic event and my own dubious share in it, I could not suppress a strong desire for revenge upon the cowardly assassin. Nor was I alone in these feelings. Lowering brows met the gaze on every hand, and deep-toned, vengeful mutterings filled the air. For many a mile this bitter spirit pervaded the captives, but ere we reached our journey's end our own wretchedness engaged our whole attention. Our feet were blistered and swollen and our suffering from this cause alone was great; but there was another and greater misery in store for us. There was no water to be had and we were soon famishing from thirst. And again, many among us had eaten nothing since the day before and these began also to experience the dreadful pangs of hunger.

The midsummer's sun still beat full upon us; his furious rays falling like molten lead upon our brains, and the road became even heavier as we labored along. And thus were we forced to march, all through that dreadful day and far into the night. What a welcome sight when at last we saw the flickering lights of the enemy's camp-fires, and how joyful the thought that we must soon hear the command to "halt;" a command which had it been given beneath the shadow of the gallows' tree would still to us have been welcome. No weary travel-stained adventurer, longing for rest, ever crossed the threshold of his luxurious home with more gladness in his heart than filled ours as we entered the stronghold of our enemies. A feeble cheer, half a sigh of relief actually struggled for expression to our parched lips as we stood still once more, tottering and catching at each other for support. Some among us would, perhaps, never know liberty again; none of us but anticipated months of wretchedness and misery, and yet the half articulate cheer we uttered was the voice of sincerity itself, for each who uttered it had told himself "Whate'er betides, I've known the worst." Some of the men sank to the ground at once and begged piteously for water; but this was not given us till we had been told off, like so many sheep, to see if any were missing. After this they brought us water, every drop of which might have come from Paradise. Every gulp was a new life, since each would have given his life for a single swallow. It was pitiable to see the famished wretches quarrel over the buckets as starving dogs over a bone, and to see with what savage avidity they gulped down the life-giving fluid. Had they known each drop to contain a subtle poison they would nevertheless have quaffed their death as if it had been nectar. Ah, truly there was enough of suffering there to atone for many a sin. The very thought of it parches my throat to this day, and by the same token it has made me too dry to say another word at this sitting."

CHAPTER VI.

We slept that night in "Stringer's" stable, nor could the softest bed of down have rendered our sleep one whit the sounder or sweeter. The sun was high in the heavens when I awoke, and great was my surprise to hear the occasional booming of cannon in the distance.

It was some moments before I could collect enough of thought to wholly comprehend my situation. A dull pain, more like a heavy weight, pressed upon my brain and completely bewildered me, but soon I began to form a clearer idea of my surroundings. My fellow-prisoners lay around me piled upon each other in all the "abandon" of extreme fatigue; just as they had sunk down a few hours before, when conscious of nothing but the sublime sensation of slumber stealing over their tired senses, they had resigned themselves unresistingly to its influence. They were still asleep. Not tasting of that lighter repose, (the recuperative draught which nature nightly sends us), but drinking deeply from oblivion's cup; a sleep the very counterfeit of death; and indeed I might well have fancied myself in that monster's grim presence, were not the breathing of my companions audible enough to dispel the delusion. A suffocating steam arose from their heated bodies and scarcely able to breath, I climbed upon a stall and put my face to a small opening to catch a breath of the pure atmos-mosphere from without. The cool air invigorated me greatly, and being in no hurry to forgo so much enjoyment I lingered there, looking wistfully out upon freedom.

I had just satisfied myself that the camp was almost entirely deserted and that the firing came from the direction of the city, when a gruff voice admonished me to "git out o' that," and looking down I beheld a sentinel with his piece presented toward me.

"What harm can I possibly do by standing here, my man," said I; "I am only catching some fresh air."

"Might catch more'n fresh air if you don't git," said the fellow, handling the lock of his musket menacingly.

"But I'll suffocate below here."

"Suffocate and be d—n," said he, bringing the musket to his shoulder.

"Miserable bondage," I cried as I sprang from my perch to the ground; "miserable bondage that denies a man even breath enough to fill his lungs."

"Might I be permitted to suggest," said a voice at my side, "that any addition to the present uncomfortable state of the atmosphere, in the shape of caloric, might add to our discomfort."

"I should have little fear of such a disaster, sir, if impertinence were calculated to forestall it," I rejoined, not deigning to notice the speaker.

"In what shape shall I administer the antidote then?" continued he with a low chuckle.

"In any shape you please," I replied, "so long as it proves effective."

"Let us try then. In the first place take off your coat; in the second, make a fan of your hat; thirdly, sit down or lie down as I do, and lastly, think of everything on earth but one thing—the heat."

"Very good in theory, not worth a cent in practice."

"But I have tried it."

"And I do not choose to."

"Acknowledge that you have a very bad temper."

"Which might be tried too severely, sir," I quickly rejoined, turning angrily toward the speaker, whom I was dumbfounded to find was none other than my friend 'Slippery Frank.'

"McPherson," I cried, "forgive my hasty words; I did not recognize your voice," and walking forward I shook his hand warmly.

"Oh, I was sure of that," said he, with a laugh; "I rather enjoyed your mistake. Sit down; it is rather better near the earth, which to a degree is cool. Bad enough anywhere, however, one might imagine 'Hades' to be only a foot or so below us."

"Not only steaming hot, but impure," I said; "what in heaven's name will become of us if we are left thus much longer?"

"We will not be, I think. They must bring us food before long, and the opening of the door will help our condition greatly. Besides, I am in hopes that then, seeing our condition, they will be humane enough to remedy it."

"I trust your hopeful conjectures may prove correct," I rejoined, "for this is a little more than I can patiently endure."

"What a day was yesterday," said my companion, musingly, "I confess I am not so much pleased with my adventure as I expected to be."

"You told me yesterday that your captivity was voluntarily brought about by yourself."

"Yes, I put myself purposely in the way of it and I now occupy the position of a spy, by compulsion This must not be long, however, for I must see Ledbetter before this time to-morrow. How, is the question."

"I fear you are over sanguine, sir," said I. "They

are watching every rat-hole in the building, as you
have seen."

" Perhaps I m ; and yet I have done it before, but,
hist, they are unbarring the door; remember, I am
farmer Speers."

The heavy oaken door was now unbarred, and while
several armed men guarded the entrance a large tray
of biscuits, a dish of fried bacon, two buckets of
water, and several large vessels filled with steaming
coffee, were brought in and spread out upon the
ground. While this was being done McPherson and
I, the only two upon our legs, stood as near to the
door as possible and drank in the delicious fresh air
which poured through the entrance; nor were we
modest in the matter of explaining our wretched
condition and of appealing to the humanity of our
captors to the end that it might be bettered. A
gruff answer or two was all that we got for our pains,
however, and the door slammed in our faces almost
as soon as it had been opened.

" This is inhuman ; it is brutal," I said, turning
away in disgust; " what of your predictions now,
friend Speers ?"

" D—n," he muttered between his teeth, while he
stamped the unconscious earth with his feet to vent
his anger.

" Becoming rather interesting," said I, with a feeble attempt at pleasantry.

" O, ho ! that is your humor, is it ?" said the other
with a sickly smile ; " you are right. It is much better than to rave, after all. Ridicule what is unpleasant to us and it loses half its poignancy."

" We certainly have the advantage of 'anything we
can laugh at," I replied; " but come, let us break our
fast. There is nothing so calculated to help a man's
feelings, whether bodily, or mental, as a full stom-

3

ach. See, these biscuits are by no means bad, and this bacon is done to a turn. My dear fellow, 'there is a sweet in every bitter.'"

"There's no sweet in that bitter, I'll be sworn," said he, as he made a wry face and shuddered, after swallowing a mouthful of the unsweetened coffee. "Taste that, and deny the adage ever after."

"On the contrary, I should be but the more firmly convinced of its truth."

"Pray explain yourself."

"Certainly. You say the coffee is bitter; now this proves its strength, and weak coffee is worthless. The very bitter, therefore, is sweet in disguise."

"Balderdash," said McPherson; "give me undisguised sweets then. But listen: the firing is more rapid now; do you notice it?"

"Yes; and by the way, what is your explanation concerning this irregular firing?"

"Merely feeling Ledbetter's strength, nothing more," said he.

"Do you think so; and why?"

"The force is too small to attempt anything more; Ledbetter is too well fortified for that; and, besides, Negley's men are scattered all over the country. Two-thirds of them are out foraging; the camp is merely a place of rendezvous selected to watch Ledbetter and hold him in check, while the coast is kept clear for the business of pillaging and capturing the unwary."

"This is part of ' Negley's' division, then?".

"Yes."

"And have they no one to fear but Ledbetter?"

"They have Morgan to fear, but as yet they do not know it?"

"Ah! May we not be rescued, then?"

"Scarcely that. The place is not suited for a surprise, and they will not fight him openly."

" You think they will run ?"

" Yes; and take you with them."

" And you ? "

" I go to Chattanooga."

" Very easy," said I, laughing—" to escape first and
swim the river after."

" And yet I will do it," said he.

"Nay," said I. " I do not doubt it ; I am only
curious to know *how* you will do it."

" Oh, that must depend upon circumstances," he
returned, as he strode away in a thoughtful mood.

One by one, the prisoners now began to awaken,
and to hasten eagerly toward the meal which had been
so unceremoniously served, and ere long quite a crowd
had gathered around it. Having eaten all I desired,
I sought again for McPherson whom I soon found,
leaning against one of the stalls and conversing with
a man wh'm at a glance I recognized as the same
who had so generously helped along the feeble old
victim of yesterday's tragedy.

" Here he comes now," said McPherson, as I
walked up; then turning to me he continued, " our
Irish friend here was just speaking of your narrow
escape of yesterday."

" Bedad," said that individual, extending his hand
to me, "it's Barney O'Hare as never seen a narrower,
sir. Sure I thought you were gone entirely."

" A close call," said I, shaking his proffered hand,
" and what on earth saved me I cannot tell."

" They're quick, these farmers, sir;" said Barney,
looking admiringly at McPherson, " may be he didn't
bounce on the dirty spalpeen ; and may be he didn't
lave as quick as he came."

"What mean you," said I looking from one to the other, "can it be possible that"—

"It's truth I'm telling you, sir," interrupted the son of Erin. "Barney O'Hare's eyes niver desaves him."

"Am I to understand from this," said I, turning to McPherson, "that I owe my life to your generous interference?"

"McPherson answered not a word, but the Irishman executed a series of nods, evidently intended as an affirmative answer to my query.

"Speak," said I, looking steadily at the scout, "tell me in plain words whether or not I owe you my life?"

"I disturbed the fellow's aim," he said; "otherwise he might have hit you."

"My dear friend," I said, not without emotion, "let me thank you most sincerely. I might have known that some one had interposed in my behalf; and yet, strangely enough it never once occurred to me. It is not likely that I can ever repay such an obligation; but if chance—"

"Balderdash," said McPherson, interrupting me with his favorite expression of dissatisfaction. "It was nothing—say no more about it," and thrusting his hands in his trousers pockets, he whistled a tune and walked away.

I turned to the Irishman then, and plied him with questions, curious to know every particular of the generous action, but Barney was not so well informed as I supposed.

"It's little I can tell you, sir, after all," said he; "I was looking at the fellow with the pistol, and scraming murther, win all at once, a body bounded by me, and lit on tap of him. Then I heard the report, and the ould man fell."

" And this is all you know ?"

"Divil a more, sir; but if you are not above a piece of advice from an honest man, I'd say look sharp for that villain. Shure he's the devil's own, sir, and he'll be after murtherin' you behind your back. Sorrow bit of a chance he'll give you, sir, and don't you forget that same."

"Thank you, Barney," said I; "your warning shall not be unheeded."

I had scarcely spoken when the unbarring of the door again attracted our attention, and I was not a little surprised to see an officer and two privates enter, closing the door behind them. A conversation in a low tone now took place between the former and one of the privates, and immediately afterward my own name rang out clear and sharp.

"Here," I said, stepping forward and confronting the officer; "what do you wish of me, sir ?"

" Ah, ha ! you are the man, are you," said he, eyeing me sternly, and immediately afterward he began, in a lower voice, to read from an open letter which he held in his hand. His words were not intended for my ears, but my senses being keenly on the alert I was enabled to catch some of them :

" Tall, large ; black moustache, hair * *; eyes * handsome * *; age * *; slight stoop, etc., etc. Very good description; pretty accurate, and you are the man, are you ?"

" I am the person whose name you called," I said, " what would you with me ?"

" Oh, you will find that out soon enough, I fancy; quite a shrewd looking young chap; and now for your friend. What name did you say, Douglass ?"

" Speers, Colonel—Jim Speers ; yonder he stands."

" Fetch him up, then, and be quick about it, for this place is as hot as h—ll."

The private called Douglass now advanced toward McPherson, who was standing some distance from us, and I immediately heard the loud voice of the supposed farmer in angry protestation.

"Go to the devil!" cried he; "I am safe enough here. Why in the thunder do you want to move us. I tell you, I'd rather stay among my friends, as hot as it is, than go outside among you blamed Yankees."

But in spite of all this he was brought to where we stood and unceremoniously handcuffed—an indignity which I myself was made to share.

"Now march them out and, mind you, guard them well," said the officer, throwing wide the door; "they must not escape, d've hear?"

"They will not escape *me*, Colonel," said Douglass, and there was so much bitterness evident in his low, sarcastic voice, that I looked quickly at him and recognized the Sergeant who had figured so ingloriously in the tragedy of the day before.

A vague feeling of uneasiness took possession of me, but careful to conceal any emotion of this nature, I assumed an air of unconcern and returned the fellow's insolent leer with a smile of contempt.

"Good morrow, brave knight," I said; "is it possible that you wear a private's uniform after your noble exploit of yesterday? You should have been promoted to a captaincy at the least."

"Go to h—ll," he said, "and shut up. You'll sing another tune soon."

"Oh, you dirthy villain," cried Barney, who walked up in time to interrupt the contemptuous reply I was about to make; "sure it's a nate lick I could give you this minute. Look out for him, your honor—look out for the blackguard; divil a scruple there is in his murtherin heart, the thafe."

A roar of laughter followed these words, which were accompanied by a series of warlike gesticulations; and amid the confusion which followed, we were led forth into the open air. Not for long however, were we destined to enjoy the sense of freedom, which unrestricted sight and action afforded us, and which was none the less pleasurable because it was unreal; for hardly had the angry voice of the Irishman died away, when, having walked toward the centre of the encampment, we were halted before a tent, and ordered to enter. Why we were brought here was a puzzle to us then, and it is a puzzle to me to this day. Having entered our new prison, our handcuffs were at once removed much to our joy, and this was another mystery to us.

"Good," said McPherson, when we were alone, " I am just one hundred yards nearer to Chattanooga;" and he flung himself at full length upon the hard earth—the only flooring to the tent. A few moments later, he was tasting of what habit had enabled him at any moment to command—a refreshing sleep.

CHAPTER VII.

I began at once to explore my tent, but there being literally nothing to discover, I soon wearied of a search so barren, and flinging myself beside my snoring companion, I became a prey to gloomy reflection. The occasional booming of a single cannon; the measured tramp of our guards, one at each end of the tent; the loud regular breathing of McPherson, and now and then the sound of a bugle, faintly heard in the distance, all these fell upon my senses with saddening effect. Visions of home and friends; of places I had visited; of scenes I had witnessed; of pleasures and of sorrows, crowded before me in quick succession. Visions that at another time and under different circumstances, would each have held some separate pleasure to bestow; or else such tempered sadness, as softens rather than wounds the heart; but now as if the shadows of a dark future were casting their sombre colors upon the picture of the past, they brought with them no pleasure. It seemed rather that they had come to bid me a last farewell, than to brighten the gloomy prospect before me.

A vague sense of impending danger poisoned my every thought, and in spite of all my efforts to the contrary I grew momentarily more nervous and uneasy. I tried in vain to sleep. Hardly would I close my eyes when some horrible dream would cause me to start and shrink from—I knew not what. And in these half-waking fancies, two faces always appeared: the demon-like countenance of the man Douglass, and, in vivid contrast, the angelic features of my

mother. The one passion-distorted, fiend-like; the
other serene and peaceful; the one on some terrible
purpose bent, and the other ever ready to thwart it.
At length I closed my eyes, determined no longer to
struggle against what seemed decreed I should endure,
and scarcely had I done so ere I fancied I saw my
mother's face looking into mine. The dream, if
dream it could have been, was as vivid as life. I heard
her gentle breathing; I felt her breath softly fan my
cheek. Then distinctly I heard her lips frame the
one word, " beware ;" and with an arm outstretched,
she pointed with her finger toward the entrance of
the tent, while her figure slowly retreated, backing
away from me. Unable longer to endure this, I
opened my eyes and arose to my feet. The vision
was gone ; but there in the doorway, his eyes gleaming
with hatred, and fixed intently upon me, was the
hated and hateful face of my enemy, Douglass. An
illy suppressed cry arose to my lips, and staggering
back, I clutched at the canvass wall of the tent for
support. In an instant McPherson was at my side.

"In heaven's name what ails you, man," he cried,
looking with wonder about him ; "you tremble in
every limb. Have you seen a ghost ?"

The question made me start anew. It was the
same that I had put to the French barber but a few
nights before and under circumstances not very unlike
the present.

" A ghost," I said, "a ghost; by heaven man, you
have very nearly hit the mark; for I saw my mother
as plainly as I now see you ; I heard her speak in her
own familiar voice as plainly as I have just heard you,
and she has been dead these many months."

" Hum," said McPherson, " 'tis strange, but I was
dreaming something of the sort myself; I wish I had

a drink," and for the first time I knew that he was superstitious.

"But this is not all," I continued, "I am completely unmanned, and as soon as I shake off this horrible spell I will tell you more. I must believe that yesterday's hardships, coming so soon after my illness, were too much for me. My brain is in a whirlwind."

"When you begin," said McPherson, coming nearer to me and speaking in a lower tone, "be careful and not raise your voice too high—look there."

Following the direction of his arm I saw the outlined figure of a man standing still just outside of the tent.

It could have been none other than Douglass.

"That man again," I whispered, "I tell you McPherson, the earth is too small to hold us both, unless one or the other be six feet below its surface. The one purpose of his life henceforth is to destroy mine."

"I am afraid there is too much truth in what you say," answered he; "may not this mysterious separation from our companions be the first act of some deep laid tragedy?"

"I have thought so, nay I am sure of it, and yet I cannot conceive of such terrible hatred as this, springing into life, as it were, in an instant."

"The cause is sufficient for some natures."

"You not only struck him down before a multitude, humiliating and degrading him before them all, but you lost him his epaulets and the favor of his officers. He is but a private to-day, yesterday he was a sergeant."

"But you?"

"I?—oh I, thwarted his vengeance; think you he knew not who did it?" "But," continued he, "we fear him not my friend; we fear him not."

"Neither do I fear a rattlesnake so long as I can see and avoid him or give him open battle. I fear no open enemy; but what of the coward; the assassin? The man who would coolly and relentlessly work your ruin without once showing his hand in the plot. You should have seen his face as he peered at me through that door but a moment ago; I shudder yet to think of it. But this reminds me, I've a story to tell you, sit down."

I now related to my friend all that I had undergone while he was asleep, omitting nothing, and I perceived that he listened to me with more than common interest. When I had finished he turned thoughtfully away without a word.

The day was now far spent, and already the shadows of approaching night were stealing o'er the camp. McPherson sat moodily in one corner of the tent wrapt in his own thoughts, while I, equally occupied with mine, walked to and fro chafing at my confinement.

At length the night came. The firing of the cannon had ceased, and the camp was fast filling with tired troops. A little after dark a similar meal to that of the morning was brought us, but we did little more than taste it; neither being in the humor for eating. Later still our guards were relieved, and this proved the signal which was to awaken my companion into activity.

He arose and shook his massive frame as if to cast off his gloomy broodings and prepare himself for a coming struggle.

"The time for action has arrived," he said, approaching me. "If I need your help I can count upon it."

"Most certainly," I answered.

"I was sure of it. Now I am going to play a bold game; such are ever the safest, and I WILL need your help. There is no occasion whatever for me to reveal my plans; you will see all for yourself. I wish it were so you could escape with me, but that is impossible, since one of us must remain in order that the other may go. I would willingly be that one, believe me, but I have dispatches which it is my duty to deliver in person. And again"—

"Say no more," said I interrupting him; "I would not leave you here were there no such considerations in existence."

"Enough then." We will meet again, I hope, and under different circumstances. Believe me, I have taken a warm interest in you, and I wish you well. Now take this for what it is worth: Whenever you receive such warnings as that of to-day, heed them to the letter. Let the wise (?) scoff at such superstition if they will, their hearts are full of doubts while they laugh them to scorn. Who is he who dare lay claim to wisdom, co-equal with that of his Maker, by affecting a knowledge of the mysteries which rule the other world? You look at me with surprise. What if I tell you that I believe we all have some one among "the past and gone" to watch over and guide us? Why are our infant lips taught to pray "Let angels guard us while we sleep," and how is it we so often FEEL an invisible presence near us without knowing who or what it is? There is such a thing as a "guardian angel," my boy; and I even I, have mine. Your mother is yours; it is my secret who is mine. Enough that I thank God for it; enough that I believe I would have long since been dead did SHE not watch over me by day and by night."

He had spoken throughout rapidly and excitedly,

but now as if a suddenly remembered sorrow choked down his further utterance, he bowed his head upon his swelling bosom and was silent. Respecting his emotion I said nothing, waiting for him to continue.

"There," he said at length, "I have said too much already. Remember only the few words of advice, forget the rest." And without waiting for me to reply, he walked boldly to the door of the tent and hailed the guard.

"Hello, out thar," he cried, "this way, Yank."

"What's the racket, Johnnie Reb?" said the fellow, looking in at the entrance.

"What's the racket?" said McPherson, never once forgeting his assumed character; "what's the racket? —a chaw of terbacky's the racket; have you got one?"

"Naw," drawled out the guard, "de'ont chew, keep quiet, why aint yer to sleep, git e'out," and he resumed his monotonous tramp without further parley.

"Can't see him very plainly," muttered McPherson, "but I guess he's not hard to manage," and with this he chuckled to himself and walked away.

I watched his further movements with momentarily increasing interest. He moved stealthily to the back of the tent and listened intently for a moment, then, as if satisfied, he began rifling his pockets of their contents. These were not numerous; a handkerchief, a piece of chewing tobacco, a few old letters, and a small sun-glass being their sum total. Next he took off his coat and laid it aside. Then doffing his hat he took from its inner lining a small slip of white paper, and carefully placing this among the letters, he tied the whole into a bundle with his handkerchief. This he shoved into his trowsers' pocket while he threw his hat on the top of his coat. Again he approached the back of the tent and listened once more breathlessly. My interest in his movements now became intense, for instinctively I knew that the decisive moment had well nigh arrived. A single feeble ray from an adjacent camp-fire struggled through the small opening at the door, and this with a gorgeous full moon afforded a light whose imperfection increased the mystery and heightened the interest of the moment. McPherson now approached me, and producing a small flat package, carefully wrapped in buckskin, he held it towards me.

"This," said he, has saved my life more than once. It is keener than a knife, and more silent, and held at a man's throat it will inspire more terror than all the sabers and fire-arms in creation."

So saying he unwrapped the parcel and disclosed a razor.

"Good Heavens man," I cried, "this is horrible; you do not mean me to—"

"Certainly not," said he interrupting me, "nobody's throat shall suffer; but it will help me to escape nevertheless. Here take it, for 'tis in your hands it must serve me, and now farewell. In a few moments more I shall be either free or—dead."

I grasped his hand warmly. "Farewell," said I, "you take with you my sincerest wishes for your success and welfare. You have given me no particular 'role' in this drama, but I presume I shall be 'prompted.'"

"When the curtain rises," said he, catching my humor, and pointing to the canvas door of the tent, and a moment later he had, for the second time, boldly hailed the sentinel.

CHAPTER VIII.

The events of the next few moments transpired much more rapidly than I can relate them.

"Se here, Yank, I'm powerful bad off for that ter-backy, darned if I ain't," said the scout when the unsuspecting guard had answered his summons. "Now I'm willing to pay for it. Just you look at this. It's worth ten dollars greenbacks, five hundred Confederate, and I'll give it for a single chaw ter-backy."

More from curiosity than with any intention of striking a bargain, the man approached near enough for the other's purpose. With the rapidity of light-ning the powerful right arm shot out and the muscu-lar fingers closed with a vice-like grip upon the throat of the unwary sentinel. He was given no time to utter a single cry, nor make the slightest movement toward defence, so sudden was the onslaught. He struggled violently, but McPherson took good care it should be silently as well, for with the same motion that he clutched the other's throat, the scout's left hand had gripped his belt, and now he held the struggling guard at arms length, his feet clear of the ground. For full a minute he held him thus, while a triumphant smile played upon his features and a low chuckling escaped from his lips. There was not the slightest trace of excitement about him, but there was a merciless determination plainly legible in his whole "mien," which the struggling man soon read aright, and which caused him to forego his efforts to free himself.

"Ah, you submit do you," said McPherson coolly,

"I was afraid you would oblige me to send you to king-
dom-come or yankee-dom—or here, be still sir; off
with your coat."

But the latter command was not obeyed, for the
man being now choked into insensibility, sunk listlessly to the ground. McPherson released his grip
and immediately began to strip the guard of his
uniform coat and cap. These he himself as quickly
donned, and picking up the musket of the still unconscious soldier, he turned to me.

"Now," said he, with a smile, "your time comes.
He will soon regain his senses. Stand over him; nay,
sit upon him, and keep your hand loosely upon his
throat, ready to stifle his first cry. Show him the
razor if he attempts to struggle, and keep him so,
until you hear the hoot of an owl in the direction of
the river, THEN you may let him go. But stay, you
may use his present helplessness to good purpose.
What if you menace him into a promise to suppress
your part in this night's work. Think well of it,
you may save yourself much misery. And now, once
more, farewell; I only await his return to life to
venture forth."

"Farewell, and success attend you," said I, "but
why wait for him to regain his senses?"

"I must have the countersign," said he, "see—
already he moves; at your post, quick."

I sprang astraddle of the prostrate man and grasped
his throat, while I held the keen blade of the razor
close to his face. I had not long to wait, ere a feeble sigh escaped him and he slowly unclosed his eyes.
A shudder passed over him as he comprehended his
situation, and he closed his eyes again without attempting to utter a word or make a single motion.

"Lie quiet, my man, and you shall not be harmed,"

I said, and I added no menace seeing it was altogether useless.

"The countersign, quick," said the scout, placing the fixed bayonet of his own musket against the fallen man's breast—"quick, I say, or by Heaven—"

"The star of the south is settting," said the sentinel in a feeble voice.

"Thank you for a lie," said McPherson, and noiselessly but quickly he bounded from the tent and left me alone with my prisoner.

Each moment now seemed an hour, an hour would have seemed a life-time. My heart beat against my breast as if trying to burst from its confinement and follow the footsteps of the friend, for whose sake it was undergoing all the agonies of suspense. My every nerve was strung to the highest pitch, and I listened with an eagerness, painful in its intensity, for the least unusual sound, that might betoken alarm or pursuit. Nor were my fears without foundation. I well knew that if recaptured and in a new character, the daring scout would be carefully searched, and the finding of dispatches upon him would seal his fate as a spy. Nothing occurred, however, to increase the fears which already racked me. The measured steps of the one sentinel without and the other sounds—very few and indistinct they were, for all that host was sleeping—served rather to increase, by contrast, the stillness of the night. My prisoner all this time lay beneath me with half closed eyes, and with a listless submission I little anticipated. This, perhaps, was less from fear than from the extreme exhaustion which succeeded his violent struggles. Two minutes must now have elapsed since my friend had left me, and believing he must by this time have safely passed the pickets, I began to breathe

more freely. I listened now with all my former
eagerness for another sound, that which would pro-
claim his freedom, and scarely had I concluded that
I might at any moment expect the welcome signal
ere it came with a distinct and exultant quiver, dis-
pelling my fears and filling me with a sense of happiness, from which even the gloomy uncertainty of
my own situation could nothing detract.

"There," said I to the prostrated man, as I released
him, and sprung to my feet; "there, do you hear
that? What means it, think you?"

"I can guess," said he, as he slowly raised himself
on his elbow and began to nurse his swollen throat.

"No need to guess," said I, "I will tell you. It
means that for the sixth time since the war began
'Slippery Frank' has been captured and has made
good his escape."

"Ha! it was he, then?"

"Certainly; I have no wish to conceal it now. And
you know him, do you?"

"That I do; and I am not likely to forget him,
either," said he, pointing significantly to his bruised
and swollen throat, which, in truth, was a sight to
see.

He now arose slowly to his feet and took a step
toward the door. I made no effort to hinder him;
seeing which he stopped and said, with a smile: "I
presume I may go now since your purpose is accomplished?"

"Yes," I answered, "go and arouse the camp and
have me put in ⬤ns, and the rest of it:—go; I only
wonder you have tarried so long already."

"Possibly I have a purpose, sir," he answered, "are
you ready to listen to a proposal?"

"Certainly," I said, "if it be worth the trouble; go on."

"It may prove beneficial," said he, still smiling. "I mean mutually beneficial, of course."

"Indeed?"

"I would not be likely to propose it otherwise."

"I should think not. But first tell me how it is your friend outside is so quiet?'

"Why, he is as deaf as a post; did you not know that?"

"Know it; how should I have known it?"

"And yet you dared what you did—the other knew it then?"

"I have no reason to think so; in fact I am sure he did not."

"Well this is strange," said he, looking thoughtfully before him; "but," he added, raising his eyes to mine, "but mayhap the devil takes care of his own."

"Oh, we were silent enough," said I, "when there was occasion for it; after he is safe I care not how soon 'tis known."

"Nevertheless, my friend would have heard you had he not been deaf; but listen: You guess, of course, that I will be court-marshalled for this, or that such a thing is at least probable; you know, also, that you will be loaded with irons and otherwise roughly treated for your part in it."

"Go on," said I, "I begin to comprehend you."

"I half intended to propose something of the kind myself, that is if I understand you aright."

"Oh, I guess you do," said he; "my plan is simple. Neither of us will know how he got away, this will clear us both—see? In twenty minutes' time the relief guard will come and before then all must be arranged. I must get a log or something to throw his coat over and to put his hat upon, understand; the imperfect light will deceive them, and I will take care they look in. I must also get myself another coat and cap and another musket. But to do all this I must leave you, see?"

"It is all plain enough," said I, "and I agree. Lose no time, if you have only twenty minutes you must use them well."

"Yes, but I must leave you. Will you stay till I return, that is the question?"

"You need not fear," said I; go, I will not leave, you have my word."

"That will do, then, I'll go and trust to luck to find what I want," and so saying he noiselessly left me.

In a very few moments he returned. All had gone well with him, he said. He had "lifted" a coat, cap and musket, and in lieu of a log he had found a bunch of "brush," which was just the thing.

"Now, see," he continued, "I lay the coat over the brush, like this, and put the hat on, like that. I spread the tail of the coat out wide enough to cover a man's legs and there he is sleeping snugly, see?"

"A master-piece of work," said I; your wooden nutmegs pale into insignificance beside such ingenuity as this."

"Now," said he, not noticing my remarks, "you lie quiet beside it and feign sleep. I will see that the officer looks in, and when all is quiet again just you fling that rebel's coat and hat in one corner and the brush in the other and all will be as nice as you please, see?"

"Exactly, sir; I will do as you say."

"And you wont 'peech' will you?"

"No," I said with a laugh, " I will not ' peech.' "

"All right; I reckon I'll leave you now. Good-night ?"

"Good-night."

He left me and walked outside, where he stood lis-tening for a few moments. Finding all quiet he re-turned to the entrance and cried out, "Say !"

"Well, what is it ?" said I.

"They're not coming yet."

"Very good; and what of that ?"

"Oh, nothing. Say, I like you."

"You overpower me, sir," I answered, laughing.

"And I would like to do you a good turn," he con-tinued.

"Nothing easier," said I, while a sudden ray of hope flashed through my breast.

"Oh, I can't let you go," he said, "not THAT; but you see here, will you tell me your name ?"

"Certainly," I answered; and having complied I begged for a similar consideration from himself.

"You are the man sure enough, then," he said, "and as to my name, it's ' Balaam,' call me 'Balaam;' everybody knows me as ' Balaam,' and if you were to ask for me by my other name my best friend wouldn't know who you meant, see ?"

I told him it was quite plain and begged that, as he had aroused my curiosity concerning a certain service he was anxious to render me he would proceed.

"It's a warning," said he; " you must take care."

"Take care; and of what ?"

"Oh, I can't tell you much about it, but look sharp, you have enemies."

"One of whom speaks to me I believe."

"Oh, I don't mean THAT—no. There's ONE, a sin-gle one, worse than all the rest."

I knew but too well to whom he alluded, but wishing to hear all he would be led into saying I assumed an air of incredulity, laughing and snapping my fingers at him. "Nonsense," I said; "you are mistaken."

"I swear that I am not," said he, with a sudden earnestness of manner; "I know what I am saying. If you value your life keep your eyes and ears constantly open, ESPECIALLY AT NIGHT."

"Enough of this," I said; "you either know nothing of what you are speaking, or you wish to make a fool of me. In either case you are wasting your breath."

"I dare not tell you more, sir," said he meekly.

"Then you know no more, nor will I listen further to your stupid twaddle. In short, my friend, I positively refuse to play the part of 'Balaam's ass.'" A low laugh escaped him at this, in the midst of which he stopped to listen.

"Hist!" he said, after a pause, "to your place, quick, they are coming!" and immediately he withdrew.

CHAPTER IX.

It all happened exactly as "Balaam" had predicted. The officer glanced at the two silent figures and was satisfied. Five minutes later one of those same figures had disappeared, and the other, lying with his head upon a certain coat, was courting sleep—a blessing which was not forthcoming. Not that Morpheus had forsaken me, for already was he leading me, with insinuating smile and soft, seductive touch, to his pleasant land of dreams; and the regular footfalls of my guards were growing less and less distinct as I followed. But alas, at this delicious stage of my journey I was rudely and cruelly recalled to the sterner realities of a more substantial existence. A horseman dashed at full speed into camp and drew rein with a loud "whoa!" In a moment all was confusion. Excited voices, hurrying footsteps and the sharp, clear notes of the bugle were sounds that almost instantaneously followed the advent of the courser. I listened impatiently for some chance word, amid all that deluge of articulation, which might explain the meaning of this sudden change from the calm of peaceful slumber to the bustle of hasty preparation. nor was I long in the dark.

"Hallo, pard!" said one of my guards to the other, "how do you read the signs?"

"Didn't you hear the bugle?" said the other.

"To arms, of course; but why?"

"Don't know. Here's a man might tell us now. This way, comrade; what's the row?"

"H—ll to play!" said a third voice, "JOHN MORGAN'S DOWN UPON US!"

"Attention !" cried an officer in the distance ; and immediately followed another bugle blast.

"He is coming up the river, eight hundred strong," continued the informant outside ; another courier has just arrived."

"The devil !" said one of the questioners, with a ring of alarm in his voice.

"Not the devil, comrade, but worse !" said another.

"And are we to run or fight ?"

"We are to change our position, man; think you we can fight Ledbetter in our front and Morgan in our rear at one and the same time ?"

A company of troops now hastened by completely drowning the voices, and before the sound of their retreating footsteps had died away my tent was being "struck" over my head, and at the same moment I was abruptly ordered to get out. I found my fellow-prisoners, but a few yards away, already formed by twos and ready to march, being surrounded by a small escort, the latter commanded by a young and exceedingly handsome officer.

"Where is the other ?" said this officer, seeing me come out alone.

"Gone," said I, laconically.

"Gone ? and where ?"

"First to Chattanooga, thence to Morgan, to whose command he belongs."

"What—do you mean he has escaped ?"

"I do."

"When, and how sir ?"

"You must really excuse me if I do not answer your questions," said I, smiling.

"How do you know he belonged to Morgan's command ?"

"That is no secret, sir :—did you ever hear of Slippery Frank ?"

The officer started.

"McPherson, the SPY—was it HE ?"

"McPherson, the SCOUT," said I, "the other is rather an ugly name."

"But not a misnomer in this instance," said he, and beckoning to an Orderly, he spoke to him in a low voice.

The Orderly saluted, and walked rapidly away, and we were immediately given the order to march. By a happy chance I was placed next to "Barney," my Irish friend, of the day before, who greeted me warmly, and afterward lightened many a weary mile with his inexhaustible store of quaint anecdote and sparkling mother wit. It would be pleasant to record some of these, if only for the sake of their brighter coloring, (an ingredient which this sombre-hued picture greatly needs,) but this, for many reasons, must not be. Barney, like many others introduced into this truthful history, was merely a chance acquaintance, who contributed little to the main current of its events, merely a land-mark to show its course ; a beacon to light me through the dark labyrinth of clouded memory. As such I recall him, and as such, whether regretfully or otherwise, I must also leave him. Nor need I dwell upon the details of that long, weary march. I soon discovered that a separate guard had been placed over me, an honor which "Barney" declared was but a wrightful homage to my importance. I need scarcely say that I considered it, but another ominous sign of that mysterious evil which was creeping so stealthily upon me. We heard no more of Morgan. I have reason to believe that the celebrated Scout was never within a hundred miles of us, and I cannot conceive of how the alarm, which caused our flight, was originated. A forced march of three days brought us to the Federal Garrison at Shelbyville. Here we were driven, like so many sheep, into a deserted commissary, and here began two weeks of abject wretchedness, merely to contemplate which fills me with a sickening horror to this day. We found the floor, the walls, the boxes (our only furniture) and the shelves, all filthy with a mixture of grease, molasses and flour. There was no escaping from it. We stood in it, walked in it, sat in it. We laid down and slept in it. And not for a single night, nor yet for two, but for two long, miserable weeks. And during all this time the heat was intolerable. Our food also was wretched, consisting for the most part of rancid bacon, and half-done corn cakes, and we also suffered from thirst, and from many other causes too numerous—many of them too disgusting—to mention. Most of the men fell sick. One man died with a smile upon his lips and we envied him; another went stark mad, and was turned out to wander, no one knew nor cared whither, and we almost envied him.

What a place to read men's hearts was this, where, tortured by a common evil, one cursed and raved, while another stood grim and silent at his side. Where another wept, and another moaned, and a few (alas, how few) went about among the rest vainly endeavoring to administer comfort and hope, or else they knelt, these very few, and prayed aloud, whilst— horrible to relate—curses and blasphemies drowned the voice of their supplications.

But let us not linger here, for very pity's sake. * *

At the end of two weeks sixty spectres tottered from this place of torment, (it was originally a barn, and belonged to a Mrs. Aiken,) and staggered toward the depot to be tumbled into box-cars and carried whirling away. Most of my companions fell asleep at once, but having noticed that my "evil spirit," Douglass, was one of the guard placed over us, a feeling of unrest took possession of me and prevented me from following their example. Why his presence should thus disturb me was incomprehensible at the time, inasmuch as I had often seen him watching me during the two wretched weeks just past, and never THEN had his presence caused me a seconds thought. Looking back upon that period, however, I can readily explain now what seemed inexplicable THEN, and I go about it thus : The moment that I escaped from the terrible sufferings of the past fortnight, to breath the unpolluted air and feel it fan my fevered cheeks in its rapid circulation through the train, I began to grow stronger both bodily and mentally. Excess of suffering had plunged me into a kind of lethargic stupor, from which I was now awakening, and with this awakening came renewed hope, and a fresh desire for life. These, in their turn, brought with them the natural instinct of self-preservation, and thus it was that the presence of Douglass rendered me uneasy to-day, whilst yesterday I would scarcely have noticed him. Many a look of hatred, many a smile of triumph, did he bestow upon me as we flew along toward Nashville. The contemplation of my wasted form and the many other evidences of suffering with which I was plainly marked, seemed to afford him umlimited delight, and he never wearied of enjoying it. I began really to hate the man for the first time. Before this I had looked upon him rather as a serpent in my path, a thing to be avoided for the present, and destroyed, if chance should require it, in the future ;

but now my fevered imagination, whether justly or
the reverse, began to picture him as the direct cause
of all my troubles; the master-hand which directed
every adverse blow aimed at me by fortune, and before our journey was ended I hated Douglass in dead
earnest. How I chafed at my helpless condition, and
how I longed for the time to come when I might meet
him in equal combat.

Whilst these bitter thoughts occupied my mind we
were rushing onward toward Nashville, which city
we reached early in the afternoon.

Arriving at the depot we disembarked and were
formed into line facing the penitentiary (which
frowning mass of brick was then plainly visible from
that point) and the order was given for all command-
ing officers and citizens to step ten paces to the front.
About one-half of our number stepped forward obe-
diently, leaving me, a private soldier with the original
line; but the front rank had scarcely "dressed," when
an officer giving me a sharp "rap" with the "flat" of
his sabre, ordered me to join them.

"I am neither an officer nor a citizen, sir," said I.

"Nevertheless, you will obey my orders," said he.

Still I hesitated, looking around me in that be-
wilderment which men often exhibit when at a loss
for a reason, and in this brief interval my eyes fell
upon Douglass, standing at a little distance away.
The sight of his sinister countenance fixed steadily
upon me, checked what further remonstrance I might
have made, and stepping boldly forward I took my
place in front without further hesitation. The two
lines thus formed were now marched off in different
directions, the private soldiers to the common jail and
ourselves to the penitentiary.

"Good-bye, yer honor," shouted a strongly accented

voice to me, as the two lines separated; "may the devil take your inimy's, sir; bad 'cess to them."

"Good-bye, Barney," I yelled, in defiance of all discipline, and being immediately ordered to "cease my bawling," I was forced to content myself with a leave-taking, which I wished with all my heart could have been warmer. I never saw Barney again, and only heard of him once afterward as being among the few who refused to take the oath of allegiance.

"You may murther me, bad luck to you, but you won't make me swear be your colors."

This is what he told them—at least, so the story went. * * *

CHAPTER X.

As soon as we were well within the high wall of brick and stone, which surrounded the penitentiary, the order was given us to break ranks, and we were allowed to wander where we pleased, a leniency on the part of our captors which both surprised and pleased us. In fact we were not long in discovering that an air of loose discipline pervaded the entire place, owing, I believe, to the fact that many were there confined for the reason alone of having refused to take the oath of allegiance, scarcely an offence to warrant, harsh or rigorous treatment.

Many of these also were men of wealth and high position, and of almost every variety of profession. We found there merchants, lawyers, physicians, and ministers of the gospel. The penitentiary was full of them, and like the jury who finds the prisoner guilty, yet recommends him to the mercy of the court on

cacount of his "high connections," the stern military
law-makers saw their decree enforced to the *letter*,
while they cared not for it's *spirit*. And thus it
came about that while we were kept strictly beneath
the shadow of the frowning edifice, and within the
walls that surrounded it, we were allowed to do pretty
much as we pleased. We roamed about the grounds
at will, and amused ourselves in many ways. We
lived in a separate world from other men, and in a
certain sense we were even happy. And so the days
rolled by. Every evening at roll call we assembled
and answered to our names, after which we were
ordered into the main building, where we found good
beds, and CLEAN; an unspeakable blessing of itself.
Our food was good, our health excellent, and our
spirits light and hopes high in consequence. Compared with our recent place of confinement at Shelbyville, we were living now in Paradise, and if we
thought of the future at all it was only to look forward to the time when we would be exchanged. For
my own part, I became well and strong at once. I
met some old acquaintances of my father's, among
whom was, notably, Dr. Baldwin, the famous Metho-
dist divine, whose able writings on Methodism have
been read far and wide. This amiable gentleman,
after hearing from my lips the story of my capture and
subsequent trials, at once took a kindly interest in me,
and afterward proved himself a true friend. Through
him I was introduced to many ladies, who were
allowed at stated periods—between the hours of four
and six p. m.—to visit their imprisoned lords, or sons,
or friends, as the case might be, and so was I held in
opinion above my companions.

"You are now acquainted," said Dr. Baldwin a day
or two after my arrival, "in the *select society of the*

penitentiary, and there is nothing to prevent your being quite happy. Come let me show you a thing or two."

And he did show me a thing or two. He led me through a suite of rooms, little short of elegant in their appointments, one of them being even luxuriously furnished.

"This," said the Doctor, referring to the latter, "is where we receive the ladies, and there on that piano they play and sing for us and lighten our hearts, God bless them. And here," he continued, opening a door into an adjoining room, "is what we call their 'toilet chamber,' look at it. Nonsense, you say, not even a looking glass? But hist; thereby hangs a tale. Come nearer, and I will tell you. Do you see that large table and those chairs? bare enough *now*, but at four o'clock, and from that until six, that table will be groaning under good things. Where do they come from? The ladies, sir; how do they get them here unperceived? A word in your ear—*hoopskirts*. You laugh." In truth I did laugh.

"Listen," said he again, after my burst of merriment; "there is a laughable feature about it, but only at first sight. See the risk they run, for if caught they would surely be made to suffer, and think of how they fearlessly lay themselves liable to the taunts and insults of the base-minded, to evil-speaking and slandering. And where is their reward, sir? They have none—none, save the sweet consciousness of having done a generous action. Yes, they come every day. There is a regular society, organized for this and similar purposes, and they send a committee every day, literally laden with good things."

"But, Doctor," I asked, "what can they bring in this—ah—extraordinary manner?"

"What can they bring, sir?—anything. A whole fowl, a pie, sweetmeats, wine, and the like. Why, my dear sir, yesterday a lady actually brought *a whole ham, ready cooked*, concealed beneath her skirts.* It was first wrapped in paper, then done up in a pillow case. You can readily conceive how this could be done if you but remember the immense size of the hoops now in fashion, and do you know, I believe this lady wore an extra large one on purpose. God bless her, but she could scarcely walk up the steps. Ah! you should see with what eagerness the rough fellows watch for their coming, and you should hear the ring of pleasure in their voices as they whisper to each other, *'yonder comes a hoopskirt.'*"

"This is truly wonderful, Doctor; but the ladies—are they never caught?"

"Trust a woman's sagacity, sir; caught? No, never. They come first to the sitting-room, after exchanging a very knowing look with the boys, who are waiting outside for a certain signal. Thence they go into their 'toilet room,' where they unpack and load the table and come out again all flushed with pride and success. After this they begin to bang the piano, a signal well understood, and the boys rush in and fall to, while the playing and singing is kept up to drown the noise of their revelry. My experiences since this war began, sir, have taught me, among many other things, that while there are only a moderate number of heroes among men, there are among women only a few who are not heroines. Opportunity is all that is lacking to prove the truth of this maxim. I know that it is a bold one, still, I believe in it; and besides I might say, what care I for the frowns of men so

* A fact.

long as woman smiles. Ah! I forget many things
that I should pray for, sir, but I never forget to say—
God bless the women."

"You interest me greatly, Doctor," said I; "there
must surely be a wonderful amount of ingenuity at
work here."

"So there is, sir; ingenuity born of love and patriotism. That which holds no obstacle as insurmount-
able; no peril as sufficient to stay its exercise. Had
men composed the members of this society, it would
never have lived to half its age. Of course, the very
fact of its being composed solely of women has much
to do with its success; for who ever suspects women of
intrigue? No one in this country, surely. The fact
is, my young friend, that men, as a rule, know very
little about women. "Believe me, we make
very great fools of ourselves when we say,
'a poor, weak woman,' if we mean one jot more
than her mere *bodily* weakness. They are
shrewder than men, and they never forget the part
they are playing. They are always curious, and this
same spirit of investigation, which we so often ridicule, enables them to see, and remove in time those
tiny obstacles, which, if left to grow, often thwart
our best laid plans. "But," said the doctor, "this
is a subject upon which I am wont to grow
enthusiastic, and I must check myself in time.
I will show you a woman this very evening, who possesses every quality I have enumerated, and many others besides, which you will
not be long in perceiving for yourself. She is the
head and front of this charitable society, a bright,
intelligent, noble little creature. And—hist—I tell
you this 'sub-rosa'—she is a northern lady born, and
is supposed to be a 'Yankee,' in the literal sense

5

of the word, while in truth, she is ardently southern in her sympathies. This gives her an immense advantage in serving us, but it also keeps her in constant peril. Therefore, beware how you speak to her in company with others. This is her regular evening for coming, and I will take pleasure in introducing you."

"Thank you very much doctor," said I, " I will come in later and claim the fulfillment of your promise. Meanwhile I will visit Dr. Jones, your barber."

" Yes," said the doctor, looking at my three weeks old whiskers, " yes it *would.* improve you. You will find Jones in the fifth room from here, left hand, straight ahead—good evening."

" Good evening, sir."   *   *   *

CHAPTER XI.

Following the doctor's directions, I knocked at the fifth door on the left, and was immediately told to "come in." Opening the door for this purpose, I was surprised to find that I had intruded upon the privacy of a gentleman, who, habited in gown and slippers, sat reading near one of the windows. As this was evidently *not* a barber's shop, and the gentleman evidently *not* a barber, I began to mutter some excuses for having intruded, preparatory to beating a retreat, when the gentleman astounded me by bursting into a loud peal of laughter, during which he slapped his thighs, and elevated his legs at intervals, in a manner quite bewildering.

" Pray, sit down, Sanders," said he—" I—ha—ha— —ha—ha. I will be over my fit—ha—ha—ha."

Being possessed of a very keen sense of the ridiculous, I began to laugh also, and for a few moments the old walls rang again, with the merry strain.

"Sanders," said the gentleman again, after he had succeeded in gaining a partial control over himself—"sit down, man—you must think me a fool, but did you ever—ha—ha—ha, ever read the 'Pick—ha—ha the "Pick-wick Pa—, Pick-wick Papers?"

Here the gentleman folded up his book, raised his spectacles to his forehead, and looking toward me for the first time, rounded off his enquiry by exclaiming, "the devil." He looked at me steadily for a few seconds, while his features began to twitch again, and a comical smile to play over them.

"You must really excuse," he began.

"It is I, who should," said I, and having got so far, we both burst into another laugh, which delayed explanations for some moments longer.

"I took you for my friend, Tom Sanders, sir," said the gentleman, gasping for breath, after his last exertion—"well, this is a lark."

"I fancy *my* mistake was a more grievous one still sir," said I, "for I took you for Dr. Jones, the barber."

"You have made no mistake at all then," said he, "for I am Dr. Jones. Have a chair sir."

"But you cannot be Dr. Jones, the—."

"Oh, I see," said he, "you wish to be shaved?"

"Exactly, sir, and if I have blundered—."

"But you have not. Sit down and I will explain."

Being thus pressed, I took a chair opposite the jolly doctor, and composed myself to listen, while he, checking off each sentence with the index finger of his right hand (as the pen) upon the palm of his left hand (as the ledger), and with a degree of loquacity, seldom if ever rivalled, began, continued, and ended thus:

"Now, sir, you are a stranger, you therefore do not know me, so far so good. Now, I am Jones, M. D., *outside*; that is, anywhere else but here; Jones, B. D., *inside*, or here; you follow me? M. D., *medical* doctor, B. D., *beard* doctor; (my own invention, and not bad I think), ha, ha—do you see?—you do?—good. You wish to be shaved—you come to me as all the others do—not that I am obliged to shave you—*no*, sir—but because being fond of surgery, and having no subjects to work upon, I take to the razor. There's amusement in it; there's art in it. You scrape as near to the skin as possible without cutting the patient, you make him actually wince, sir, without drawing blood. My dear sir, there *is* art in it—as I told my friend Sanders only yesterday. We were discussing the movements at Manassas—a bloody affair that, sir, I was on the spot, the arms and legs I helped to take off on that day; astonishing—astonishing. One of the most pathetic sights I have ever witnessed occurred on that day—the case of a young man—his mother lives right here in Nashville, and has two beautiful daughters, lovely girls; the eldest a blonde, no, a brunette, and the el—I mean the youngest, has just become engaged to a *very* handsome young fellow—an officer. Perhaps you have met him Mr. —— What *did* you say your name was?"

I mentioned my name to the doctor, and ventured to hint that as I had made an engagement to meet some ladies, he might finish his very interesting narrative while he took off my beard.

"Certainly," said the doctor—"yes that was it. I never *could* remember names, sir—never. Shave you while I finish, of course, sir—of course; may I trouble you to lather your face at the basin there; sorry I

have no brush; while I get my razor and rub it up.
I find the leg of a boot sir, to answer in lieu of a
strap, which I haven't got; ah, here it is, not very
sharp I am afraid, but I will try to make it answer."

While the doctor, whose volubility never for an instant flagged, was hurrying nervously to and fro, making
preparations for his task, I had approached the basin
and wetting the soap I began as directed to lather my
face. But before I had completed this preliminary
operation, a thing occurred which I would much pre-
fer to leave untold, could its suppression by any possible means be made consistent with the strict veracity
of this history. I was still vigorously rubbing my
bristly chin, when happening to raise my head a little
I caught a glimpse of my face reflected in a small
fraction of a mirror, which, from its diminutive size, had
hitherto escaped my notice. This piece of glass had no
frame around it, but leaned against the wall with its
base resting upon a small bracket, and was almost
entirely concealed from view by a brush and comb
and several other articles of the toilet. Now, there
is nothing, I am sure, to make even a timid child
start and tremble at the unexpected apparition of his
or her image reflected in a looking-glass; and yet,
however inexplicable it may seem, certain it is, that
I, a grown man, in the full enjoyment of health, and
not given to timidity or excessive nervousness, *did*
start and tremble at thus suddenly beholding my own
image. I did more. I staggered back and uttered
an exclamation of fear, if not of actual terror; for
although I saw the glass, and fully knew that the
reflection could have been none other than my own,
yet *the face that I saw, and still seemed to see, was not
my own, but that of my dead mother.* Call it what you
will; the hallucination of a brain diseased by recent

suffering, the wild fancy of a nature naturally superstitious, but peculiarly so at this time for similar reasons; advance an hundred theories as explanatory of
this extraordinary effect produced by so commonplace a cause; but ask *me* not to select from their
number the right one. I could by no means rid myself of the nervous ague which seized me. I laughed
at a weakness I could not conceal. I stammered forth
various explanations and excuses to Dr. Jones, who
stood watching me in open-mouthed wonder; yet in
my heart of hearts I could ascribe my strange emotion to no *earthly* source. There was one desire
uppermost in my mind, which had sprung into life
simultaneously with and as a part of my indescribable
malady, and this was a desire to leave the room as
quickly as possible. It was with much haste and very
little ceremony, therefore, that I washed my soap-
besmeared face, and scarcely waiting to dry it, hurried away, leaving Dr. Jones staring after me with
such a look as he might have bestowed upon the retreating form of a madman.

CHAPTER XII.

Actuated by a desire to be alone, I bent my steps
toward my own room, or more properly toward the
diminutive apartment whose comforts I shared with
two others. Here I was disappointed to find one of
my room-mates, who for want of better occupation,
was stretched upon his bed indulging in a day dream.
This gentleman, whose name was Putnam, was six
feet three, and a very giant in strength. He had also
a heart of proportionate size to his frame, as I had

already begun to conjecture, and of the truth of which
subsequent events gave infallible proof.

"Hello," said he, regarding me through his half
closed lids; "is that you?"

It was too late to retreat, and in order the better to
conceal my agitation I made him some light rejoinder
and flung myself upon my own bed, with my face to
the wall.

"Do you intend to sleep?" asked Putnam, "or are
you about to indulge in aerial architecture? If the
latter, let us work together. Come, I had just completed a most extravagantly beautiful country residence, away from wars and rumors of wars; but,
pooh, I blow it away and commence anew. First I
lay the sills of—"

"Air," said I, with a feeble attempt to catch his
humor.

"Of air; but of cool, delightful air; not hot, suffocating air like this; and, go ahead, your turn comes."

"What comes next?" I asked.

"What comes next? Why the—let me see; well,
I don't know, confound me if I do. We will call the
house finished, and proceed to furnish it—Proceed to
furnish it?"

"It must be shell-proof," I suggested.

"And proof against heat," said he; "very good, go
on."

"The walls of gold, diamond chandeliers pendent
from the ceilings, handsome mirrors, in frames of
gold."

"Yes, and Brussels carpets a foot deep—every bit
of a foot deep, and curtains of rich—of rich what?"

"Gold cloth; we will say, gold cloth and lace."

"Fringed, you know; they must be fringed with—."

"Strings of pearls, perhaps."

"Good; excellent, and there must be sofas, *soft* sofas," said he, striking with his fist the mattress of shucks upon which he was lying.

"Aye, very soft, and—let me see; what else?"

"We will sum up the rest, and say every luxury and every comfort that heart could desire."

"Good; and now our aerial castle becomes ethereal; let us begin to people it."

"A wife," said Putnam.

"Two," said I.

"The devil," said he.

"I mean, one apiece."

"Oh; that is a gray horse of another color; but where are our cattle, man? We must have horses."

"Certainly, and therefore stables."

"*With separate stalls; at least two separate stalls, for the asses,*" said a voice at the door; and looking up we beheld Brown, our room-mate, who had stolen upon us unperceived.

"Well, for two grown men," continued Brown, after we had laughed heartily—"for two grown men:—well, I never."

"Humph," ejaculated Putnam, assuming at a single bound the air of a philosopher—"you know not at what you scoff, man. For my own part, I am thankful for the ingredient; whatever you may call it, which enables us to deceive ourselves, so long as that deception is pleasing. Nor are they necessarily fools, or "asses" either, who indulge this fancy. Why should they be; there can be no harm in it; and do we not, by building up an imaginary world around us, live for the moment in *that*, while we lose sight of *this*, with its harassing cares and trials? Thus, we not only give ourselves a sinless pleasure (which is quite

a rare thing, by the way) but we rest our faculties at
the same time. I tell you, Brown, such exercise is
quite as harmless, and to the full as refreshing, as a
pleasant dream."

"Give *me* the sleep," said Brown ; "fools, idiots."

"Oh, very well." said Putnam, shrugging his shoulders, "nevertheless everybody—."

"Everybody is an ass then," sneered Brown.

Before Putnam, whom the other's 'crustiness' had
somewhat nettled, could make a reply, there came
to our ears, the soft, mellow notes of a distant piano,
at the first sound of which, Brown bounded to the
glass, adjusted his cravat, put a few touches to his
hair and whisker, took his hat under his arm and
hurried away without a word.

"Always hungry," said Putnam, looking at me
with a smile—"always hungry and crabbed. He will
be the first there, I warrant."

"And I must not be far behind him," said I rising,
"for I have an engagement to meet Mrs. Nickolson."

"She is there," said Putnam. "Listen, that is her
voice, I know it well. She would sing Dixie if she
dared," continued he after a pause, "but no, it is
'Home, sweet home'—ah, me—ah, me."

These last monosyllables, uttered in a tone so full
of sadness, opened before me, in an instant a volume
of serious reflection ; and as, guided by the music, I
took my way along the cold, damp passage, my mood
was by no means suited to the gaieties of the draw-
ing-room.

It is a good and a beautiful thing in our nature,
that oftimes, when separated from home, and the
countless influences for good, which continually surround us there, a single word, a note of music, a scene,
the song of a bird, or the odor of a flower, will cause

a host of sweet remembrances to rush upon us, filling us for the moment with a tranquil though regretful happiness, and softening us into better and purer beings. And the greater the doubt of our ever renewing those dearest of all earthly ties, as in times of war, the oftener and the more easily are we moved to contemplate them. How very thankful we should be, that we are one and all, susceptible to such influences, especially when we reflect that at such moments, and only at such, the good angel may hover quite near us, without fear of the evil contact. Occupied with such thoughts and not willing to banish them, yet equally unwilling to give way to the emot'o is which they awakened, I hesitated at the door before opening it to pass in, and it was at this moment that a rough hand was laid upon my shoulder. A sudden chill flashed through me like an electric shock, and even before I could turn to look upon him I had *felt* his presence, and knew that Douglass was beside me. Returning the malignant leer with which he regarded me, with as much hauteur and contempt as I could concentrate into my gaze, I drew myself proudly up, and folding my arms across my chest, waited for him to speak.

"Oh, you need not put on airs, my young cocksparrow," said he, "your comb will soon be cut. Ha, ha, ha, only a day or two; only a few hours longer, and then—vengeance; sweet, sweet vengeance."

He stopped, while he shook with suppressed rage, and a half smothered cry of exultation escaped from between his firm set teeth; a cry like the laugh of a fiend.

"Why don't you speak?" said he again—"why don't you beg for mercy—ha, ha, ha, for mercy. Oh, hate, hate, and sweet vengeance. I could take it now for I am armed, but no, I must wait; and I can wait.

The rope, nothing but the rope for you. Where will be your pride then, eh, eh? Oh, curse you, curse you. You have thwarted me at every turn; you have heaped upon me disgrace and humiliation;＿but *you* know what you have done, during all this long time since we first met. No need to remind *you* of it all; curse you; oh, curse you. Liar, thief, slanderer, your time has come."

The man by this time had worked himself into a perfect frenzy of passion. His bosom heaved, his eyes seemed about to burst from their sockets. his lips were bloodlessly white, and he trembled in every limb. Up to this time I had said not a word, having maintained throughout this bitter tirade, the exact position I had assumed upon first beholding him; and the longer I kept silent the stronger grew my determination to remain so. For more than one reason this seemed my wisest, if not my most satisfactory course. If I opened my lips I would lose my self-control and strike him. This done, I would be thrust into a cell and loaded with irons, a result which, in all probability, Douglass was then working to bring about. This consideration alone would have outweighed any desire I might have felt for punishing the man, but as he proceeded, a new and equally powerful motive, added as it were, the seal to my lips.

"Give you rope enough and you will hang yourself," I whispered in thought; "and not only may I hope that you will reveal your plans of vengeance and thus forearm me, but that you will utter words which will throw some light upon the *true* source of the hell-born hatred you bear me."

"You thought you were rid of me," continued Douglass, who had only stopped to catch his breath.

"You thought you were rid of me, now didn't you?
Why don't you speak, I say? Are you not going to
beg for your life? Do you know you are about to
die?—dog—hound—speak, I say. Oh, you don't believe it; you defy me; you ain't afraid; very well,
but when you are dead—dead and buried; ha, ha, ha,
how then; *who will protect her then?* Ha, you
start; you grow pale; no you *don't* start; you *don't*
grow pale—oh, damn you, damn you. Who will
shield *her* from my vengeance *then?* I say; you know
what that vengeance will be. *You stole her from
me,* did you?—you—slandered me did you? you lied
on me—you—but never mind—your time has come,
and *I* will have her; yes *I—I.*"

Still I kept silent, not however without a powerful
effort. Insult heaped upon insult made my blood
boil, and I longed to strike him to my feet, but I
would not. There was that in his speech too, (it will
tax nobody's sagacity to comprehend what,) which
made me think of other matters than his bitter words,
and perhaps this to some degree dulled their poignancy.

"Nothing will move you then," continued Douglass, "will a knife in your heart move you? Will a
rope round your neck move you?—we shall see—we
shall see. And when you are dead—dead I say—*she
shall pay—.*"

Here the music, which had hitherto drowned his
voice, abruptly ceased, and Douglass hearing footsteps apparently approaching the door, slunk away
into a side passage; his last act being to shake his fist
and spit at me. For a moment I stood quivering
with passion, inwardly cursing the fate that had rendered my passive behavior necessary; but by degrees
anger gave place to prudence, (we seldom possess the

two at one and the same time,) and I began to feel
more satisfied with my course. "He shall pay dearly
for this at another time, I muttered, but for the
present I have acted wisely. I have not only served
myself well, but I have defeated any plan he might
have laid to get me into immediate trouble. And
again—his mysterious words. It is not then solely
my action on the day of my capture, which has created
the remorseless hatred he bears me. Can I have
crossed him in some other way without knowing it,
or can he be mistaking me for another?"

Having taken a turn in the passage, and having
stumbled upon no answer to these puzzling questions,
I suddenly remembered my engagement, and shaking
off as nearly as I could, all thought of Douglass, and
of the myriad evils in the shape of mocking devils,
which danced around his very name, I assumed an air
of unconcern and entered the reception room.

CHAPTER XIII.

Dr. Baldwin met and introduced me.

"Ah, my young friend," said he, extending his
hand; "come in. I have been expecting you for
some time. You are much improved since you—but
you have *not* shaved, eh? What, Jones out? Why
that is strange, for he is something of a hermit generally. But come, we will go the rounds. First,
here is the judge—Judge Marchbanks, (his father
a particular friend of mine, Judge,) and next, Miss
Fitzsimmons, and Miss Callahan, Mrs. Kent, Mr.
Horlbeck; but you know most of the gentlemen, and
here, last but *not* least (except in size) is the lady of

whom I spoke to you this morning, Mrs. Nickolson; (a particular young friend of mine, ma'am)."

I had already heard enough of this lady to feel more than a passing interest in her, and I now beheld her with something of curiosity.

I noted at a glance, first, that she was rather below the middle height of woman, but symmetrical in figure; and secondly, that she was rather plainly though neatly dressed in black, and that her complexion was exquisitely clear, almost transparent. Her manner of receiving me was hearty and unaffected in the extreme, and she wore a smile so sweet and winning as to captivate me at once. There was that in her smile too, which seemed to give emphasis to her unassumed cordiality; as if its brightness lit the way to her heart, that I might read there the truth of what she uttered.

Though by no means a homely, she was equally far from being a beautiful woman. Her features were clearly defined and regular, but too prominent for feminine beauty. Her eyes were dark, expressive and penetrating; her lips thin and firm set, denoting determination, and her forehead high and very prominent. Her chief charm lay in her manner. Apart from a soft sweet voice, a distinctness of utterance, (always pleasing) and a wholly unstudied expression, (too carefully selected speech often falls with a chilling effect upon the listener, renders him ill at ease and makes him wonder how much of it is really meant,) apart from all these and many minor charms, for which there is no name, unless the word "feminine" embodies them all, there was a subtle attraction about this lady not easily described. A "something" in the atmosphere which surrounded her which lulled the senses and filled one with a feeling of quiet enjoyment. A kind of mesmerism, so to speak; as if something of her own peace and purity of heart communicated itself to those around her. Whatever this nameless attraction was, (and I would like to call it the delightful essence of her own chastity and goodness,) it held as in a spell all who came near her. No one approached her but with a sensation of growing pleasure, which only reached its climax at the thrilling touch of her extended hand; no one left her but with lingering step.

"I feel as if I know you already," said she : "Dr. Baldwin has spoken of you so often and with so much kindness. Take a seat and tell me something of yourself, you *do* look as if you had suffered; but who has not? Ah me, how I wish this cruel war was over."

I sat down beside her as she bade me, and for a full hour I resigned myself wholly to the enjoyment of her society. She monopolized the conversation, nor did I once feel the remotest desire to "edge in a word." Even to this day, as I glance backward upon the picture of my chequered life, I recognize this, my first hour with Mrs. Nickolson, as among the brightest spots upon it, which shine forth here and there to mark the moments of pleasure; like stars through a storm-cloud. Her conversation led me away from every distressing topic. If she spoke of the war at all it was only to recount some recent victory for the Confederate arms, of which I had heard nothing. At such moments her eyes fairly sparkled, her bosom heaved and her cheeks flushed, while she poured forth her triumphant story in one unbroken stream of simple yet touching eloquence. Eloquence not of the lips, but that which is far more beautiful —of the heart.

I listened spell-bound. I became filled with a far greater devotion for my country and her glorious cause than I had ever felt before, and my inactivity began to weigh upon me with new and painful acuteness. Mentally, I registered a vow to escape at once, and once free, to wash out in the blood of our common enemy, the— what I now deemed—positive disgrace of having thus far quietly submitted to captivity. These resolutions were formed while Mrs. Nickolson—having for a moment turned to the piano—was running her fingers idly over the keys, as a signal to the revellers in the adjoining room to cease their noisy clamor. This signal she often found it necessary to repeat, and it never failed to have the desired effect. Even in the midst of a boisterous fit of laughter, the very first note of the piano would produce an instantaneous silence; cutting short the mirth in a ludicrous manner. Having established silence, she again turned to me and laughingly said :

"They are a parcel of boys, sir; every one of them. Afraid of me too—of poor little *me;* well, I *never.*"

I did not join in the low, silvery laugh which escaped her after saying this, but scarcely waiting for it to cease I said abruptly :

"Mrs. Nickolson, I must escape."

"Ah," she said, not so much as changing her expression; "I saw it, you know. There was a new light in your eye when I turned from the piano, which I construed into something of the sort. Escape?—why surely you must."

"But how, madam," said I, "how is the question?"

"Mind," said she, placing a finger upon her lip to enjoin silence, "you must be careful. And you really mean to escape, do you?"

"I do, madam, if such a thing is possible. I have

too long remained in careless submission to this bond-age, forgetting all the while that my country needed even my weak arm. But I am no longer forgetful of my duty. Your words have opened my slothful eyes and awakened within me a new energy. I must escape, and at once; but again recurs the puzzling question—how?"

She remained in deep thought for some moments, with her eyes fixed upon the carpet at her feet. At length, raising them to mine, she said slowly:

"It cannot be done just yet, and you must abandon the idea, at least for the present. There are others besides yourself to be considered, who have been longer in captivity, much longer than you have been, and you must be content to await your turn. Your own efforts would avail you nothing, be they never so bold and daring. Stratagem alone can succeed, and you cannot even exercise that to any fruitful end without the co-operation of a friend. No, you must be patient and leave it all to me. You look sur-prised."

"Leave it to *you*, madam? I scarcely understand."

"Not understand? You have not thought. Do you not know that for the sake of the cause I love, and for those who uphold its principles, I have con-sented to live a perpetual *lie?*—to *spy* upon and *betray* those who believe me true to them, whose hospitality I share, and who represent the very land of my birth?"

(Here her eyes filled and her voice became tremu-lous.)

"Do you not know," she continued, "that for the sake of those principles I have recklessly hazarded every tie that binds me to life? The love of friends, of kindred, wealth, position—everything is held as *noth-*

6

ing by all who think as I think ; who love as I love.
Knowing then what I am, you can easily conceive the
immeasurable advantages my position affords me.
Nay, this knowledge might teach you more. It might
enable you to guess (knowing the depth of my love
for you and your cause) to what desperate lengths I
would go to serve you ; and it might teach you also,
(knowing the energy and ambition which such love
begets) how well I have employed my time in shaping
these advantages to serve you. How can you feel surprise then, when I say leave it to me ?   Think you I
cannot, or will not serve you ?   Why, I tell you, boy,"
said she, brightening up and bustling hurriedly toward the piano, "I have already 'done the State some
service.'   There is a little memorandum here in my
pocket-book with *fifty-four names* upon it; the names
of your brothers in arms whom, during the past year,
I have helped to escape from captivity.

   "It is a fact," said she, pausing with her hands suspended above the keys, "it is a fact, and whenever
my life of duplicity weighs heavily upon me, my life
of *deceit and falsehood, of heartless treachery and
calculating baseness—*"

   "Hold, my dear madam," said I, "you are doing
yourself a vast injustice—"

   "God knows, I hope so," said she, brushing away
the tears which had again filled her eyes.   "I hope so,
and I always bring myself to believe so, if I but read
over these names, each one of which recalls in regular routine some touching story and its joyful sequel.
And when I reflect that were my actions wholly wrong
such universal success could never attend them, I am
comforted.   'God smiles upon and furthers my feeble
efforts,' I softly think, and every feeling of doubt
vanishes at once."

Her fingers descended upon the keys as she concluded, and a moment later she was singing as if the
slightest care were stranger to her breast. I will not
attempt to describe the emotions which filled me after
listening to these frank avowals. Let it suffice to say
that my admiration for this character, every beautiful
trait of which stood self-revealed, amounted to something akin to adoration. The blending of so much
that was heroic, yet gentle; energetic, yet prudent;
firm, yet tender and sympathizing; a mind and a
heart so wholly generous and self-sacrificing, I am free
to confess I had never met with before; and I now
contemplated them with something of awe. Nor can
I think this estimate of her overdrawn. It is possible,
that if called upon then, instead of now, to express
my opinion of her, I would have hesitated ere I gave
full warmth to my admiration; but as subsequent
events only confirmed my first impressions, I would
be doing both her, and myself an injustice, were I at
this time, one iota less devout of my theme. But I
neither ask nor desire you, my worthy reader to indorse
what may seem unto you an extravagance. I am re-
cording *facts*, you know, of which my feelings and
impressions are part and parcel, and if these fail to
please, I must submit to, however much I lament,
your displeasure. In no wise can I hope to afford you
any great amount of amusement. If I but help you
to forget now and then 'that little balance at Reug-
heimer's,' or 'that small matter at Klinck & Wicken-
burg's.' That Mrs. Green wore a new bonnet at
church last Sunday which, (although a positive fright),
did make your wife's last winter's hat look shabby
alongside of it; or if perchance I bring you to forget
that your arrears at——the club, (blessed institution)
have been overdue these four days, in consequence of

which you have not lunched there in *three;* if but for
a moment, I say, you forget these, or any similar considerations, in following me in my adventures, it is
all I can hope for, and quite enough to content me.
For believe me, it is well worth the trouble—so argues
my own experience—to turn the pages of the very
driest of chapters, so long as in doing so we are made
to forget the alarming discrepancy between our ex-
chequer and the myriad demands upon it.

And now, but one more word and I am done with
prosing. The character of Mrs. Nickolson, who lived
and still lives, is not an isolated one. That she was
among the fortunate few whom opportunity served
in pursuing her noble work, is undoubtedly true; but
that she was exceptional in either her love of country, her self-denying spirit, or her courage, is as undoubtedly false. Where is the veteran soldier who
cannot point you to more than one incident of his experience, in which the devotion and patriotism of woman shines forth in deeds of heroism, among the very
brightest which stud the annals of the late war?
Deeds the more to be honored because achieved in
secret, and of a consequence, unalloyed by a single
thought of personal distinction or glory; deeds seldom rewarded and as seldom even recognized. Mrs.
Nickolson, then, is only one of many whose devotion,
whose willingness to serve, and whose personal prow-
ess were to the full as great as hers, but who lacked
the *opportunity* to achieve the same amount of good
as herself. While I, therefore, in my humble walk, do
honor to this lady's name, let me not forget the many
others whose generous deeds are covered by the veil
of modesty. Because I owe my life to her, let me
not forget her unknown sisters, who have saved other
lives than mine.

CHAPTER XIV.

Although all personal intercourse with my newly made friend was at an end for that evening, yet was I destined, before she departed, to witness a certain ceremonial in which she played a conspicuous part, and which afforded me a still greater insight into the beauties of her character. This was the distribution among the prisoners of certain pairs of socks, hand-kerchiefs, collars, and even shirts, and also of certain small packages, carefully wrapped, and said to contain tobacco, snuff, etc. These the president produced from a well-filled pillow-case which, during our interview, she had kept concealed beneath the piano. It is scarcely necessary to say of the donees that they were rough, uncouth fellows, a motley crew at best, and by far more familiar with the smell of gunpowder than with the perfume of "eau de cologne;" yet were there none forgotten, each receiving in his turn some little token of the watchful care and generous love of their acknowledged bene-factress. And these gifts were not offered haughtily, or condescendingly, but each was accompanied by a smile and a manner whose perfect candor disarmed at once every lurking feeling of diffidence or reserve. Thus she knew them all personally; called them by their names; shared with them their hopes and their fears, and, as far as she was able, supplied their wants. There was something quite beautiful, and unspeakably touching, too, in the way in which these gifts were received. In order to avoid any display of gratitude, the good woman hurried through the ceremony, scolding all who dared to loiter near her even for a moment; yet was there time enough for each to offer his thanks, and in a manner, too, which more than once brought the tears to my eyes.

"God bless you, lady," one would say in husky accents, while the next to follow could only *look* his thanks through eyes that swam; and the next, mayhap, would grasp her extended hand along with the package it held, and cover it with kisses; or fall upon his knees, and with all the hallowed reverence a worshipper might vouchsafe to some holy relic, press to his lips a convenient portion of her dress. This scene affected me greatly, nor do I believe it is ever destined to fade from my memory.

I saw Mrs. Nickolson depart with a feeling of actual sorrow, and I roamed listlessly about for hours afterwards, a prey to gloomy reflection. Even after I had retired to rest, my thoughts were busy with the events of the day, each particular of which kept constantly recurring with a persistency that precluded all possibility of sleep. Nor, strange to record, did I find the retrospect in the least degree enjoyable. A strange uneasiness had taken possession of me, a feeling which I could not define, nor, combat it as I would, could I master. It was not so much a regret for the fleetness of my season of happiness, as a vague fear that some evil consequence might flow out of it, as if some dire penalty were attached to so much enjoyment. I reasoned with myself in vain. I even sat up in bed to be sure that I was thoroughly awake, and checked off the "pros" and "cons" on my fingers; but while I became satisfied that my one hour of pleasure could directly cause no calamity, yet my undefined fears did not leave me. Towards morning I got up and walked about for an hour, after which I

felt keenly the need of rest, but no sooner had I lain
down again than I perceived the utter uselessness of
attempting to sleep.   My eyes seemed propped open,
my troubled faculties refused to desert me.   I arose
again and walked to the window.   The first streaks of
dawn were now visible in the east, and as I perceived
it, I felt my heart sink with an odd and crushing hopelessness.   I sat down and buried my head in my
pillow.   One of the sleepers moved uneasily and I
started at the sound, unable in my extreme nervousness to account for it.   I moved once more to the
window and peered without.   The daylight was now
fast approaching, and in the uncertain light each
object I beheld seemed distorted and misshapen.
Whatever I looked upon, it was sure to move, and
with a degree of stealth that chilled my blood; and if
I heard a noise, however slight or commonplace,
my fancy was sure to give it some evil significance.
I shuddered and turned away.   "God of mercy," I
cried, "can this be madness?" and, as if in answer to
my despairing cry something darted through the window and fell upon my bed.   Trembling, I picked it
up and hurried with it to the light.   It was a small
piece of white paper attached by a string to a brick,
and upon it was scrawled in pencil the word "to-day."
I unfolded the paper and a sickening horror seized
me as I beheld the rude drawing of a coffin sur-
mounted by a skull and cross-bones; and almost faint-
ing I fell upon my bed at the same moment that a
low, taunting laugh reached me from without.   Once
again I arose and staggered to the window, reaching
it just in time to catch a single glimpse of a retreating figure as it slunk away in the semi-darkness.
"Douglass," I muttered, drawing a long breath, and
oddly enough, the belief in his presence gave me

instant relief. And so it ever is. An undefined fear, the unexplained presence of evil, is more torturing to the mind by half than the full knowledge of the direst calamity which could befall us. I endeavored now to think calmly and carefully over my situation. Taking for granted that the horribly significant missive, which I still held crushed in my hand, had come from my relentless enemy, I was not long in reading it thus: First, that my life was in imminent and immediate danger, and further that an attack of some kind would be made against it on that very day. This warning I considered as a great advantage gained. It mattered little that I was entirely ignorant of the particular kind of weapon my antagonist would employ against me, I was at least able to show him my *front*, knowing when to look for him. If he could be stealthy, I could be wary; if he (amply armed and surrounded by friends) held every advantage, I at least possessed an equal amount of courage and determination. Having canvassed the situation thus far, I began at once to "breathe more freely," as the phrase goes ; but suddenly it occurred to me that it was possible, nay, even probable, that my arch enemy would employ some other hand than his own to strike at my life ; and no sooner had I conceived this idea than I began to accept it as a certainty, and once more was I cast down, even to utter hopelessness. Scarcely knowing what I did, I dropped on my knees clasping tightly my throbbing temples, and immediately, even before I knew it, my heart lifted itself in prayer. The attitude alone had suggested the supplication, (alas, that it should have been so) but when I arose I was calmer and more hopeful. I dressed myself and issued forth. The first bright rays of sunshine were slanting along the grounds, and the fresh, brisk morning air invigorated and cheered me. Ere I

had walked many paces the sentry challenged me and
demanded my business, but having explained to him
that I was feverish and could not rest, he kindly
allowed me to continue on my way. For a full hour
I pursued my objectless walk, the mere act of motion
seeming to divert my thoughts and so assuage my
fears. Although I had fully resolved to meet my
fate unflinchingly (and I never doubted the near
approach of evil), yet had I ceased to wonder what it
was. I felt now a 'settled, ceaseless gloom,' nevertheless
I was resigned, and if I felt impatient, it was rather
from suspense than from a lack of submission. I
even began to long for the blow to fall, when by a
defiant and fearless bearing I might either conquer,
or, dying with a still unbroken spirit, cheat my enemy
out of half his revenge. While yet I pursued my
purposeless wanderings, the day had greatly advanced
and the business thereof had well begun. The bugle
summoned us to roll call preparatory to breakfast,
and with the rest I answered the signal; but I started
when my name was called, and answered as one in a
dream. I ate my breakfast mechanically, and with
such an air of abstractedness that several remarked
upon it.

"He's still asleep," said one.

"He's been carousing all night," said another.

"I rather think he is drunk," said a third.

And to each of these charges my only acklowledg-
ment was a weary smile.

CHAPTER XV.

I left the table among the first, only to continue my solitary rambling. And now as the moments flew and I found myself still unmolested, I began to grow impatient. Yes, strange inconsistency of the human heart; I grew actually impatient for the coming of an evil whose approach I never doubted, and whose coming I felt scarcely less certain would involve the loss of my life.

A distant clock struck the hour of nine. I had stopped to count the strokes, and having done so, I was about to move on again when the sound of hurrying footsteps arrested me. Looking around I perceived that Putnam was approaching me in a half run, and ere I was given time to form a conjecture as to the meaning of his abrupt visit, he was at my side.

"My dear fellow," said he, "what in heaven's name is the meaning of this report, which has just reached me, *that you are suspected of being a spy, and that you are to be tried by court-martial to-day?*"

"Ah!" said I, with a sigh of actual relief; "this is it then; at last I see his hand."

"Eh?" said Putnam, "I do not understand."

"It is nothing," I returned with a sorry attempt at a laugh; "nothing, except that 'tis a lie. I am no more spy than you are."

"And you can prove it?"

"Indeed I cannot."

"You cannot? then this is serious."

"If the loss of my life be serious."

"But, my dear fellow, you speak strangely ; you do not even seem surprised."

"No, my friend," said I, "I am not in the least surprised. This is nothing less than a plot to ruin me. I have an enemy of whom I have told you something, *he* has done this. I knew full well he was about to strike, for he even warned me, but I did not know until now what would be his mode of attack."

"Good God," said Putnam, "this is bad ; and you say he warned you?"

"Even so ; come, stroll along with me and I will tell you all."

I now told him how that all night long I had been unable to sleep, a prey to an extreme nervous depression, which at first I could not account for, but which later I had recognized as the shadow of an approaching evil. I produced the horrible warning and showed it to him, mentioning every mysterious circumstance connected with it, and I wound up by saying that I believed the snare had been but too well laid, and that I could not hope to escape its consequences ; but that I was resolved to meet my doom as became a man and a soldier.

Instead of offering me his sympathy, Putnam, to my unbounded surprise, seized me by the collar with his powerful right hand, and shook me until my teeth chattered again.

" Now, in the name of all the gods at once," shouted he, by a mere chance hitting upon a quotation to suit the occasion ; " 'pon what meat doth this our—what's his name, feed, that he hath grown so great? So great as to make a coward of you ; to rob you of your spirit, your energy and independence. Will you allow this sneaking coward to swear away your life, while you stand submissively by and mope like this, actually holding your neck for the halter? Wake up, I say; what in heaven's name will become of your old father when you are hung? No hope! nonsense—no hope! the devil."

Under other circumstances, this rough usage might have nettled me, but now, in contemplating the advice itself, I lost sight of the emphatic manner in which it was given. The suddenness and violence of his attack; the emphasis with which he spoke; his allusion to my father, reminding me of his age and helpless condition, and the sudden and sweet conviction, that there was at least *one* friend at hand, all conspired to stimulate my waning hope, and arouse me into action.

In a single moment of time, then; so susceptible are we by nature, so slight the agencies which sway us, whether for good or evil, so fickle our judgment, and so frail the foundation upon which we often build our strongest arguments; in a single moment of time, the despair which had filled my heart had flown and left it bounding with a new-born hope.

Ah, what tremendous destinies may hang upon this brief interval, "one moment of time." Even in the first story of all—that of the Garden of Eden—we may perceive this momentous yet little thought of fact. The doom of ages, the fate of millions, hung upon the few brief seconds of indecision which preceded the fall of man. In a moment our Lord was betrayed, and in a moment did Peter deny him. It consumes less than a moment to sign away the peace of a nation, and in a moment or less the guillotine accomplishes its dreadful work. In a single instant the very blackest of crimes may be committed; and, thank God for this—in an instant too, so merciful is our Master, the very blackest of crimes may be repented. What valuable lessons should we learn from these contemplations. With what extreme care and deliberation should we form our conclusions and our resolves, and how well considered should be our speech at all times and under all circumstances. *These* are the lessons He contempl ated to teach, who said: "Be ye slow to anger;" and these the precepts so beautifully comprised in the words, "Give thy thoughts no tongue, nor any unproportioned thought his act."

To Putnam I now turned, and grasping his hand in the sincerity of my gratitude, I began to thank him for his friendly interest and excellent advice.

"My dear friend," I said, "already I see my situation in a new and more hopeful light. I shall no more despair, I shall—"

"There—there," said he, suddenly tightening his grip upon my hand, "it is too late to say more; see, here they come. Never say die, remember that. I will do all in my power; I will not rest; be calm; be cautious; be firm; but above all, be hopeful; and now good-bye."

He was turning away, but at that moment and for the first time a horrible thought crossed my mind, and stretching forth my hand I held him back.

"Putnam," I said, "a single word before you go. Should the worst come, and they drag me to the scaffold, you will not let me die like a dog; promise me solemnly, that you will—"

"Hist,"- said he, trying to escape—"hist, they are here."

"Promise," said I; "if you be a man, promise me."

"I promise," said he, shuddering perceptibly—"I will do it, *if I can.*"

I loosened my grip, and he was gone. I had no

time for further thought. Not a moment in which I might have seen the magnitude of the wrong I had inflicted upon my best friend, in thus exacting from him a promise, to be true to which he must inevitably have wrecked his own happiness, and as surely have hazarded his life.

Ere Putnam had walked a dozen yards away, an orderly and three privates stepped up to where he had left me standing.

"Your name, sir," said the orderly.

I drew myself up, and gave it in full.

"I have been ordered to escort you under special arrest before the court-martial. Forward—(Dennis, you and Burch lead the way—Thompson, bring up the rear with me)—march."

I made no resistance.

Until we left the prison grounds where, of course, we were the "observed of all observers," I felt an actual delight in the thought that my steps were firm and my bearing proud. A walk of five minutes brought us to a handsome dwelling, recessed from the street, at the gate of which stood several richly caparisoned horses. This, I soon learned, was our destination. A sentinel challenged us; the orderly spoke a few low words in his ear, and the gate swung open to admit us. The sound of boisterous merriment reached my ear as we entered, and grew louder as we approached the somewhat gloomy-looking edifice. I cannot say why, but it sent a cold chill careering through my veins. At the door we again halted and the orderly went forward, leaving me with the three others. Soon, however, he returned and led the way into a large room, where the "Tribunal Militaire," was already assembled. In the single haughty glance which I threw around me as I entered, I saw a large table upon which was piled a number of hats, some belts containing side-arms, and a few swords, and around which were seated a number of officers. Immediately opposite the door, and just behind the president's chair, stood a side-board laden with decanters and glasses, explaining at once the source of the mirth which I had heard while approaching the house. Except these, the room was bare. As we entered, there was a rap upon the table, followed by a hiding of smiles behind handkerchiefs, a pulling down of vests, a whispering and a winking, after which there was a chorus of clearing of throats, an assumption of grave dignity, and lastly silence. It was easy to perceive from these and other signs betokening impatience, that the company had been disturbed in the midst of festivities very much to their liking, and that they were by no means well pleased at the interruption. There was a look and an air about the whole assembly which, to me, was painfully eloquent, and which I read thus: "A plague upon the meaningless rigmarole of a military trial. If we had not to conform to these empty formalities this fellow might have been comfortably shot without disturbing our frolic;" and I confess there was something exceedingly unpleasant in the perusal. To me it smacked of a verdict already fixed upon, of a doom already sealed.

I did not, however, allow these ominous appearances to rob me of one tithe of my firmness, and when the president commenced the proceedings by reading aloud my name, and paused, looking at me with an interrogation point in his eye, I bowed with the air of a man who was very proud of it indeed, and who was not in the least afraid of its ever getting him into trouble.

"You are denounced," said the president, "by Sergeant Douglass, of the—ah, regiment and division blurred—as a spy. The penalty, you are aware, is death," continued he, coolly folding up the paper and removing his eye-glasses. "Call Sergeant Douglass and let him make the charge."

Immediately there was a scarcely perceptible noise behind me, and glancing round, I saw the grinning face of Douglass, behind whom stood two privates, who afterwards appeared as witnesses against me. It is useless to say that, to my knowledge, I had never seen either of them, nor can I believe that they had ever seen me. Douglass made his charge in a monotonous sing-song strain, avowing that on several occasions he had seen me within the federal lines wearing their uniform and mingling freely with the troops. He mentioned several places and dates (which have since escaped me), where and when he had seen me. In proof of these charges he produced as witnesses the two privates, who swore that they, too, had seen me on each of the occasions mentioned by Douglass and under the circumstances described. The plot, I soon perceived, had been ingeniously laid, and before the somewhat prolix charges had been half made and sworn to, I saw my inevitable fate before me. The court listened with every evidence of increasing impatience, and at length the president, rapping loudly upon the table, remarked that the witnesses were consuming entirely too much time. Douglass, ceasing at this, glanced for a moment at the faces around the table, and as if he read in them an all-sufficient reason for so doing, he saluted and withdrew.

"Have you finished?" asked the president.

"I have nothing more to say, sir," said he.

"And what has the prisoner to say in his own defense?" continued the former, turning to me.

"Simply that these accusations are all false from beginning to end, sir, and that they are manufactured by an unscrupulous scoundrel, who, too cowardly to seek the reparation common among men of courage, resorts to this dastardly means of satisfying his personal revenge."

Uttering this bitter speech with all the vehemence of long pent-up anger, I looked the while straight into the eyes of my cowardly accuser, and had the satisfaction of seeing that his glan·e fell before me, and that he actually writhed in his seat.

There was a perceptible stir occasioned by this defiant outburst, and the president, re-adjusting his eye-glasses, looked at me through them long and searchingly.

"You are strangely violent, sir," said he, in a voice which betrayed not a little agitation, "considering certain unpleasant facts, which you seem to have forgotten. But where is your *proof;* nothing less will serve you here."

"And do you ask me for proof," I cried, the mockery of this demand firing my indignation and depriving me of every instinct of caution ; "you who know every circumstance con_ected with these baseless ch?rges? You, who know that, up to a few moments ago, I was not even aware of their existence. What time has been allowed me to prepare defense of any kind? There is not a shadow either of justice or common sense in such a demand, and this you well know. You both mock my helplessness and disgrace the office you hold, sir."

"Silence!" thundered the president, rising to his feet and turning livid with rage.

"I am nearly through," continued I, smiling at his wrath.

7

"You shall insult us no further, sir," shouted he again, while he reached forward and half drew from its scabbard a sword which was lying before him.

"No other power than death shall stop me, sir," said I, folding my arms across my chest and eying him coolly.

"Then death it shall be," cried he fiercely, as he drew forth the blade and started toward me. There was now a general rising from the table, and a hurried resumption of weapons. Some of the more impetuous prepared to annihilate me at once, but a few of the older officers interposed themselves resolutely between us, while an old colonel hooked arms with the president himself, and leading him forcibly aside, began a whispered remonstrance. In less time than I have consumed in the telling, the officers resumed their seats, and the president, in a choking voice, informed me that I might say whatever I wished in my defense, but if a word were uttered, coming not strictly under this head, the court would proceed to pass sentence at once.

"I have nearly finished, sir," said I. "I have only to protest against these proceedings, the indecent haste and the mockery of which dishonors your country and your flag, and insults mine. I well know that your verdict was fixed upon, even before you saw me, and that, had you dared, you would have had me shot without a hearing; and I have to say this: that the day of reckoning for each of you will as surely come as that the sun rises and sets. And as to that cowardly scoundrel whose lies you accept as truths, let him tremble, also, for whether I live or die, a terrible vengeance awaits him. Now, sir, I am ready to hear your sentence."

There was a moment of silence, followed by another

of whispering, and the president arose and said, laconically:

"To-morrow, at sunrise, and you shall have until then to decide whether you will be hanged or shot."

"I wish no time to decide this," said I. "Let me die a soldier's death."

"Take him away," said the president, and a moment later, I was being led back to prison, surrounded by a strong escort.

CHAPTER XVI.

There are periods in the lives of most men which, although they vie in importance with the most remarkable events of a lifetime, are yet remembered vaguely and disconnectedly; and especially is this the case when impending danger gives consequence to the occasion. At such moments the mighty instinct of self-preservation engages our every energy, and soon our mental faculties become clouded from overwork. Myriad plots and plans flash, meteor-like, through our brains, to be abandoned almost as soon as conceived, each bringing with it a momentary ray of hope and leaving behind it the blackness of despair. And so it is, that all these vacillations, too numerous and too fleeting to strike us with retentive force, are soon forgotten, and we remember the period and the events thereof only as a unit. The traveler, caught in a terrific storm, will scarcely forget the adventure itself, but he cannot tell you how many flashes blinded him, or how many peals of thunder shook the earth, notwithstanding that each terrific shock made him cringe and tremble at the time.

Such a period, then, and so remembered, were the few short hours immediately following my sentence. I have no remembrance that the fear of death haunted me, or that I lost hope for a single moment. The activity of my friends, and their words of encouragement, the universal indignation which my position called forth, and above all my freedom; for I was not locked in a cell, as might have been expected; all these conspired to give employment to my thoughts, and to keep them back from the dread to-morrow. I was as active as the most zealous, and to the full as cool to all outward seeming, and yet I had every reason to despair.

Putnam was one of the first to meet me after the trial.

"As I expected," said I.

"But not the rope;" said he, with a perceptible shudder; "tell me it is not the rope."

"No, thank heaven," said I, "they have promised me a soldier's death."

"A tight scrape," said he thoughtfully, "but we have been in a tighter, eh? Take courage. What a pity we can do nothing *till dark*."

"Till dark."

"I echoed the words, and strangely enough I began from that moment to look upon the coming of the night as the period which would end my troubles. I have said that I was active, and this I repeat; but in what my activity consisted I know not, nor can I say what it was that I hoped or expected to gain from it. I dined as usual, and I remember that, although every eye was turned upon me, I read in them nothing but encouragement. Many of my companions toasted me, and wished me God-speed upon my journey, each accepting my escape as certain.

After dinner, Dr. Baldwin took me aside and handed me a crisp twenty dollar greenback note. "This," said he, "may be useful. There is scarce a lock which a golden key will not open."

Thanking him, I took the note and added it to my scanty fund.

"Putnam is raising a purse for you," said the doctor. "Ah, here he is now."

"I've just seen them all," said my huge friend, walking briskly up. "Let me see, here is the list: Dr. Baldwin, twenty (he has given you his); Elliott, twenty; Dr. Ford, twenty; Judge Marchbanks, twenty; myself, twenty;—now, what had you before? Count it up."

"One hundred and sixty dollars, all told," said I, after reckoning my wealth.

"Good," said Putnam, "that will do admirably, and now we can do no more until—"

"Until dark," said I.

"At least, until after roll call," said the other.

"Do you know," said Dr. Baldwin, "that Brown has taken the oath, and was released an hour ago?"

"Is it possible," said I.

"Yes, it was I who begged him to do it, although I had reason to believe he would have done so before very long of his own accord. I wished to communicate with Mrs. Nickolson in your behalf, and this was my only chance."

"And did you send him to her, doctor?"

"Yes, and if he has succeeded in seeing her, she will be here before the sun goes down."

The doctor had scarcely ceased speaking when a carriage rolled up to the gateway.

"The reception room," said the latter, and I immediately made my way thither.

Mrs. Nickolson was not long in appearing.

"My dear young friend," said she, approaching me with both hands extended, "*what* is this I hear? Oh, dreadful, cruel war. But have you *hope*, have you *courage?*"

"Thank heaven, madam, I have both," said I, as I stooped and touched each of her hands to my lips.

"Then never despair, I am doing my utmost to save you, and can only stay to say so much. If I succeed, you shall hear from me in time, and if I do *not*— but I WILL—good-bye."

Without waiting for me to reply, she hooked arms with Dr. Baldwin and hurried from the room. I walked to the window to see her depart, and was rather surprised to notice that the gate stood ajar, and that several men, whom I took to be prisoners, were entering. I counted seven of these, and was wondering where they had been captured and what news they might bring, when something about the foremost struck me as familiar. I looked at him more closely as he approached, and soon perceived that he was indeed an old acquaintance, Willie Watterson by name. A friend, I should rather say, for although I had known him in all but two weeks, yet so slowly do the hours of adversity drag themselves away, that, in that otherwise limited time, there had sprung up a warm friendship between us. I had first met with him at Shelbyville, and had parted with him at the depot in Nashville on the day of our arrival, he to go to the jail, and I to come to the penitentiary. He was scarcely out of his teens and possessed a hearty, open manner, a handsome face, and a light-heartedness withal which seldom failed to please at first sight. I sought him out at once, and told him my sad story. As I expected, he was greatly shocked,

and his words of sympathy were many and sincere.
He made me repeat my story many times over, and
after each repetition, he poured forth a perfect torrent
of abuse upon all blue-coats; invariably winding up
by saying, "but you shall not die so—no, by heaven,
you shall not."

Shall I own that these vehement assertions pleased
me well? That I fed my hope upon these empty
boasts, and that, stranger still, I found them nutritious
and strengthening? Tell me, ye wise men—is there
any such thing as *downright despair?* At length I
questioned Watterson concerning himself and his own
fortunes.

"I have taken the oath," said he sadly; "there was
nothing else for it. I blush to own it, but I was compelled to the step by necessity. What that necessity
is, I cannot tell you now. There are nine of us, all
told, who obtained our release this morning, and as
most of us had friends here, we were allowed to visit
the penitentiary. I swear to you, my friend, that I
am ashamed to look you in the face, but if you but
knew—"

I stopped him abruptly, for a sudden hope had
flashed through me. "Hold," I said, "you must have
had a pass—let me see it."

He looked at me steadily for a moment, and as my
meaning struck him, he turned pale.

"I understand," said he, in a low voice, "but it is
of no use—a part of it is printed."

"But the signature, let me see *that.*"

Without a word he produced the pass, which I
snatched eagerly from him; but a single glance at it
was sufficient to crush my hope, for there was a seal
upon it which I saw at once, would defy every art of

forgery. Slowly, and sorrowfully, I handed it back to him.

"Without the seal, it would be useless," I said.

"Yes," said Watterson, "but I have thought of something else. Look you," he continued, with increasing agitation, "this pass may save you yet. *It is made out for nine men, and on our route hither, two strayed away.* Do you see—do you understand?" cried he, as with trembling hand he grasped my shoulder; "*you can pass out as one of those who did not enter.*"

Heaven help me. I had sustained my courage up to this moment upon absolutely nothing; but now, that a reasonable chance of escape presented itself, I grew in an instant as weak as a child.

"Go," said Watterson, who had actually to support my tottering limbs; "go—lose not a moment. See, already they are assembling for the roll call. Answer to your name, then hasten away and disguise yourself. Borrow another suit, and *shave off your beard.* We can only remain here until seven o'clock. Rouse yourself, my dear friend, and be active, without displaying haste; be bold, but cautious; lose no time in *action*, but lose sufficient in *thought*, that your deserving haste may be the greater; go, and meet me at the gate as "Jackson Williams."

"I will do as you say," said I, "your thoughts are inspired. But why must I call myself Jackson Williams?"

"Because such was the name of one of the men who strayed away."

"Enough," said I; "I will be there."

I was barely in time to answer to my name, having done which, I touched Putnam's arm and led him to our room. Once there, I told in a few words of what had passed between Watterson and myself, and before I had yet finished, the honest fellow began to strip himself of his clothes. I verily believe that had I not stopped him, he would, in his blind generosity, have divested himself of every rag he wore; but having hinted to him that his garments were at least a dozen sizes too large for me, he began slowly to don them again with an air of much disappointment.

"I will find you a suit," said he, hurrying away, "meanwhile go to Dr. Jones and get a clean shave."

I found the doctor at home, puzzling his brain over a problem of chess.

"Walk in," said he, "draw up a chair and look at this—whites to play and check in three moves."

"Come, doctor," said I, "I am in something of a hurry; shave me clean—quick."

"Eh," said he, "there is really not a particle of soap."

"Never mind, sir, if you can make it appear that I shaved a day or so ago so much the better, and I fancy the absence of soap will help to produce this very appearance."

The doctor looked his amazement, and although he prepared to do as requested, his movements were so slow that I was obliged to acquaint him with a portion of my story in order to arouse him into greater activity. To produce a pair of scissors and to crop me close was the work of a very few moments; after which followed the scraping with the very dullest of razors, a process which was a little less than torture. Although the doctor was but a few moments in completing his task, yet did it appear an age to me, fretted and impatient as I was, and when I arose from my chair it was with a feeling of relief seldom more sincerely felt. After washing my face,

which felt strangely diminutive and unfamiliar between my palms, I hastened to the glass to note the
change made in my appearance. I confess I was not
prepared for so great an one. The bronzed soldier
with fierce moustache and long beard had become a
smooth-faced youth, the upper half of whose physi-
ognomy was sunburnt enough, but whose cheeks
were as fair as a girl's.

"This will never do," said I, turning to the doctor,
"the contrast between my upper and lower face is
too striking. I will be detected at once."

"I have thought of that," said he, "and happily I
have the remedy at hand. Resume your seat for a
moment."

While speaking the doctor had produced a coffee-
pot, into which he now plunged his hand and drew
forth a quantity of the dripping sediment. This he
rubbed upon my cheeks, and having given it time to
dry he brushed away the particles which adhered and
announced with every evidence of satisfaction that I
might now defy recognition.

"Remember, however," said he, "that soap and
water or even a vigorous rubbing without either,
will obliterate your artificial bronze; look."

Thus speaking he held the glass before me, and
I was greatly pleased to note how well this simple
device had worked.

Taking a hurried farewell of the doctor, whose kind
words at parting I felt to be sincere, I hurried toward
my room. As I hastened along the gloomy passage the
sudden remembrance came to me of my first visit to
Dr. Jones. This remembrance, and the reflections it
conjured up, took me at a bound to the scene with
the French barber in Chattanooga, and brought me
back again to the present, and to the fact of my now

beardless face. Many a time before had I pondered deeply upon the mystery of the first two of these occasions. Many a time had I asked my inmost self if indeed it could have been my mother's spirit who had twice prevented me from carrying out the same intention, and who once had warned me against the man who had indeed proven himself a subtle and remorseless enemy, but never had I found an answer to the puzzling queries. Never, until now, when of a sudden the mystery appeared revealed before me. The sublime, the beautiful thought of a mother's love, living even beyond the grave, overwhelmed me with emotion, and involuntarily pausing I raised my hands and cried :

"It is indeed you, my mother, who thus watches over and protects me. I see it all now, how that you have interfered to save me, for had you left me to myself, I had been helpless at this crisis."

I brushed away the gathering tears and resumed my hurried way.

Neither difficult of acceptance nor unpleasing is the belief, that those who loved us here are still permitted to regard us with affectionate solicitude after the insatiate grave has claimed them ; and whatever the doubts which have come to me with twenty years more of life, certain it is, that at the time, I believed most fervently in the theory.

I found Putnam awaiting me. A long coat of coarse, dark stuff and a black slouch hat had been procured, and these I proceeded quickly to don.

"I would not have known you," said Putnam, as he assisted me in dressing, "had I not anticipated the change in your appearance. I think there can be no doubt that you will escape. Leave the city at once and make directly for the nearest Confederate lines.

Try and 'press' a horse, better not trust to the railroad ; and now farewell and good luck attend you."

Only a fervent pressure of the hand and a look straight in the eye (neither devoid of eloquence), and we parted. I have never seen him since, nor do I even know if he be still alive, but I have neither forgotten his exceeding kindness, nor the generous warmth of his friendship.

It was now nearly seven o'clock.

As I passed out into the passage I stuck my enormous hat well back upon my head, and assuming an air of swaggering self-sufficiency, I left the building and mingled boldly with the men outside.

Dr. Baldwin passed me, and sidling up to him, I whispered my name and my farewell in his ear. He seemed perplexed, but I dared not venture upon an explanation, and I left him, not even waiting for his parting blessing, which otherwise I am sure would have been forthcoming. I now sought for Watterson, whom very soon I found surrounded by a group of his friends. I had my doubts about joining the group, but Watterson set at once the question at rest by calling out :

"Hello, Jackson, this way."

"Our time is nearly up," said I. "Good-evening, gents." The men bowed and echoed my salutation, but none seemed to recognize me, although there were those present whom I knew and who knew me well.

"This way a moment," said Watterson, leading me to a little distance. "The guard at the gate has just been changed," said he in low tones; "but the fellow relieved still lingers there. We must wait until he leaves, or we must get him away by some means ; do you understand ?"

"Yes," I answered, "he alone knows that only seven men entered the yard."

"Exactly; and this is my only misgiving, for your disguise is perfect."

"We have five minutes or so," said I, "but by all that's lucky, we do not need them, for the fellow is already moving away."

"Good," said Watterson, glancing toward the gate; "now I will rejoin these men, and as soon as the coast is clear, I will give the order to march."

As Watterson left me, I looked once more eagerly towards the gate. The relieved guard, with coat unbuttoned, cap in hand and a musket trailing behind him, was loi'ering lazily towards us, pausing now to exchange a word with an acquaintance; now to unfix his bayonet and sheathe it at his side, now to listlessly kick at a pebble, or to stretch himself and gape. "Will the idle fool never be gone," I muttered, stamping the earth in my impatience, and longing to catch him up bodily and hurl him out of sight, a feat which, in the intensity of my impatience, I felt as though I could find the strength to accomplish. "If I could but get behind you with a bayonet," I thought. But he moved no faster for the wish, and it seemed an age before he dragged himself up the steps and disappeared into the building. Watterson lost no time after this. The six men who had accompanied him were already at hand, and after a hurried farewell, in which I joined or seemed to join, we marched toward the gate.

What a war of emotions waged within me now. The fear of discovery made my heart throb fit to burst through my ribs, and fiercely did I struggle to preserve the appearance of calm. Happily for me this struggle was short-lived, for before I had time to think twice of my situation we were at the gate.

"This pass is made out for nine of us, as you will see, sir," said Watterson to the sentinel, "but one of the nine left us before we got here."

The fellow took the pass and scanned it narrowly for full a minute. It seemed with difficulty that he read it at all, but at length as if satisfied, he slowly moved toward the gate and, holding it open, nodded for us to pass out.

I shall not attempt to describe the swelling emotions of my heart as I emerged from the deep archway of the prison-gate and heard its heavy bang as it closed behind us. The very madness of delight seized upon me, and it was with difficulty that I could restrain myself from bounding away at the top of my speed and crying aloud in the ecstasy of my conscious freedom.

CHAPTER XVII.

For all his youth and frivolous gayety of manner, Watterson possessed a cool head and a wise. Before we had yet compassed a full block from my late prison, he recommended that we should part company.

"If by any evil chance your escape is immediately discovered," said he, "you will, of course, be sought as one of this company. Let us say farewell, then, or at least let us branch off by twos at this next corner."

The wisdom of this advice being self-apparent, we acted upon it at once—Watterson and myself making our way toward the "St. Clouds," and the others scattering in various directions.

"Now," said Watterson, when we were alone, "so far so good. Those fellows are all true. Not one but would die rather than betray us. For the present, then, all is well; but what of the future—what are your plans?"

"My plans?" said I. "Except that I have a vague notion of joining my corps as soon as practicable, I have formed no plans. I tell you, man, this glorious consciousness of freedom which I feel is far too delightful to be banished. I will not think now, lest I break the spell. Look you, Watterson, my boy, did you ever feel like a balloon—eh? What are you laughing at?"

"Well, no," said he, chuckling heartily; "I cannot say that I ever have. Nevertheless, I do not doubt that *you* do, for you certainly possess at least two of the ingredients which should produce the feeling."

"Name them," said I; "what are they?"

"Elasticity, for one," said he, "for you walk as if there were springs beneath your feet, and you keep me in a half run to keep up with you."

"Well; and the other?"

"Gas, because you are remarkably fluent of speech, and there is nothing in what you say. But here we are at the St. Clouds. Hold! we must register."

"I presume we must."

"And have you thought of an *alias?*"

"No, by the Lord, I have not; but lead the way; anything will do."

Watterson made straight for the desk and registered his full name, after which I took the pen from him and wrote off boldly,

"Dick Mays, Gallatin, Tenn."

"Come, Dick," said Watterson, who had looked over my shoulder, "let us have some supper," then turning to the sleek-headed clerk, he continued: "My friend and I will spend the night. Will you have us shown to a room?"

The clerk touched a gong, and as if by magic a neatly dressed black appeared. "Twenty-two," said the clerk, throwing him a key.

The fellow grabbed it and turned to us with a low bow.

"Baggage, gentlemen," said he.

"None," said Watterson.

"Yes, sir; this way, sir, please," and he led the way upstairs.

Once in our room and the servant dismissed, I turned to Watterson, and with something of amazement, asked what he meant by saying we would spend the night there.

"Where else would you spend it?" said he.

"What! shut ourselves up here?"

"Not at all. We will have supper, and afterwards a cigar and a stroll. We will follow our fancy, or yours rather, and amuse ourselves in any way which pleases you; but when we are sleepy, here is our bed."

"The devil," said I; "to be recaptured to-morrow and shot the next morning at sunrise? I confess I like not the notion."

"What would you do then?" said Watterson.

"I—I would leave this; I would fly; I would—"

"When, how, and whither, pray?"

"Well," said I, somewhat crest-fallen, "I have not thought of that. I presume I must trust to luck."

"A very poor dependence, let me observe, if you adhere to your resolution and refuse to think, for what is luck but the fruit of cool, deliberate calculation—of energy and tact? Employ these, and be guided by the result, or listen to my advice and follow it."

"Go on," I said, "the cooler the head the better the judgment."

"Then listen. Your escape, if not already known, cannot long remain a secret, this you must admit; very well. Once known, extraordinary precautions will be immediately taken to prevent your leaving the city, but notwithstanding these precautions, when morning comes and you are not retaken, ninety-nine men out of every hundred will believe that you *have* outwitted them all and left the city. This belief will cause them to relax their vigilance, orders from headquarters to the contrary notwithstanding; do you follow me?"

"But to-night," said I; "they will search every hole and corner of the city."

"Every hole and corner in the *outskirts* of the city," returned Watterson, "but not in the very heart of it; and least of all *here*, where fifty officers take their meals daily, and half that number regularly board."

"By heaven," exclaimed I, jumping up—"friend Watterson, you have made me bolder than I am wont. But after all," continued I, reflecting, "perhaps it is this very boldness which you believe will constitute my safety. A man in my position, however, never feels safe unless he is on the go."

"Forgetting all the while," said Watterson, "that he is making tracks by which he may be followed. But I have not yet finished, this only brings us to to-morrow morning."

"Exactly; say that I am not facing a platoon when the sun rises, what then?"

"This," said he. "By the luckiest chance in the

8

world, I have here a pass to Wartrace, Tennessee, for myself and a friend. This friend is to meet me at the train leaving the city at eight o'clock in the morning; but as he has nothing to fear in remaining here, he will readily consent to lending you his name and giving you his seat in the coach. I am sure he will not hesitate to do this; but even if he should, you can still be off, for in that event you can travel as Willie Watterson. And now that all is settled," continued he, giving me a friendly slap on the back, "let us hurry down to supper before those Yankees bankrupt the larder. Listen to their noisy clamor."

Watterson threw wide the door as he finished speaking, and we descended to the supper room. Here we found seated at the various tables at least a couple of dozen officers of every rank and arm of the service, who were laughing and jesting at a high rate of enjoyment. By a happy chance a waiter led us to a small side table where, seated with my back to the company, I enjoyed a hearty meal; the peril of my situation giving an indescribable zest to my appetite.

CHAPTER XVIII.

Those who are pleased to follow me in these confessions will probably not complain if I but glance at the events of my first night out of prison.

In common parlance, Watterson and I "made a night of it," and if this hackneyed phrase be capable of many constructions, their number could scarcely exceed the variety of the feints we made at enjoyment. With fool-hardy daring we ventured into highways and byways, into saloons and billiard rooms, into cafes and public reading-rooms, and everywhere our loud talk and noisy laughter drew special attention to us. We had reason enough, heaven knows, to pursue the very reverse of this conduct, but had we listened to prudence our pleasure had vanished, for it was in the indulgence of this same dare-devil spirit that we found our chief enjoyment. Youth, in all the pride of its conscious strength and courage, is seldom so happy as when sparring with danger. The inborn love of adventure, possessed by us all in a greater or less degree, lures us on to grapple with peril, merely for the sake of the enjoyable excitement afforded by the struggle.

Compared with this favorite sport of the young and adventurous, the fascinations of the gaming table are as nothing. On the one hand we stake our gold, and to lose means only to cripple our fortunes; while on the other we stake our lives, and to lose means—death. For these reasons then, and not in the exercise of any profound art of strategy, did Watterson and I recklessly and in many ways expose ourselves to momentary detection, and for these reasons also, do I look upon this night as one of the most intensely enjoyable of my life.

Shake your venerable heads, ye sage old gentlemen; pucker your lips and frown to your hearts' content; but when you have done, glance backward for a moment upon the season of your own youth, and if you *must* pronounce us young fools, you will at least forgive, for I warrant me you will find something in the retrospect to plead for us.

The business of the night, which was to furnish myself with a much needed suit of clothes and a pair of boots, was soon concluded. A few steps from the "St. Clouds" brought us to Church street, and once here we were not long in finding a boot and shoe store.

"Hold a moment," said Watterson, as we entered the latter, "let me put a flea in the clerk's ear;" and so saying he left me and stepped forward to where a young man lay at full length upon the counter. As Watterson approached, he raised himself into a sitting posture, and looked suspiciously from one to the other of us.

"You have nothing to fear, sir," I heard Watterson say, as he reached him, and after this followed a brief half whispered colloquy. Whatever the words, their effect upon the clerk was magical. Uttering a hurried "eh?" he sprang from the counter and approached me at a half run.

"Certainly, sir, certainly," said he, "with the greatest pleasure," and reaching me he grasped my hand, which he shook warmly, and continued, "proud to meet you, sir, honored sir, and you want—why certainly, sir, step this way—with the greatest pleasure, I do assure you."

I was not a little surprised by these manifestations of kindly interest vouchsafed me by one whom I had never met before, but attributing it all to the effect of Watterson's "flea," I followed the clerk to the rear of the establishment.

"Now, sir," said the clerk, removing the lid from a box filled with cavalry boots—"now, sir, here you are—help yourself."

Thanking him, I selected a pair of number sevens and drew them on, after discarding my well worn "brogans."

"How much, sir," I asked, surveying my feet with something of pride.

"Oh, nothing, nothing at all, sir, I wouldn't think

of charging you—wouldn't think of it. Wish I could do more for you, sir, do indeed. Hope you will get safely away from these Yankees, sir—damn 'em."

"How," said I, "so then my friend yonder has been telling tales out of school. But," I continued, "I have no apprehensions on the score of either your fidelity or your prudence, sir, and now allow me to thank you heartily, and bid you good evening."

"What in heaven's name did you tell the fellow," I asked of Watterson, as soon as we had left the place.

"Oh," said he, laughing heartily, "only that you were a confederate officer, high in rank, and that you were here on a most important and perilous service; that you were short of means, and that you very much needed a pair of boots; that is all."

"A very good joke," said I, "but, my dear fellow, is there not a dash of imprudence in it?"

"Not at all," said he, "I knew the fellow's sentiments."

Next we entered a clothing house, where Watterson repeated his strategy—if so it may be called—with equal success, and I soon found myself fitted out, "from top to toe," in a new, and what appeared to me (more perhaps from contrast), a rich and handsome suit. To the man who possesses a very nice sense of gentility, a rent in his garment is a direct and severe wound to his self-esteem; a patch upon his boot is no less a scar upon his respectability, and never, unless he be faultlessly dressed, does he feel in its fullest and grandest sense, the proud consciousness of the possession of all those ennobling attributes embodied in the one word of "gentleman." Nay, I may even go farther, and assert that a heart like this, if covered by a ragged coat, cannot feel its full competence of courage.

"I feel myself in every respect twice the man of a moment ago," said I to Watterson, as I stepped out of the store arrayed in my shining apparel. "As I cast aside my worn and faded garments I felt as if the act relieved me of a burden of humiliation, almost of shame, and as I drew on these, as if I clothed myself once more in my natural pride and self-respect. Aye," I continued, as drawing myself up, I stepped out more boldly; "pride and self-respect, the twin brothers which stand ever in the vanguard of all the higher qualities of manhood."

"Excuse me," said Watterson, "but are you rich, are you a prince in disguise, have you great expectations, or have you ever stormed a battery single-handed? No? then what the devil have you to be proud of?"

"Excuse *me*," said I, catching his meaning and not half liking it; "I speak not of the pride which is puppyism; nor by 'self-respect' do I mean that covetous self-love which in my esteem is the very basest of all sordid qualities. I speak only of that pride which glows in a man's heart, like the embers on the hearth, kindling noble emotions and warming generous aspirations; of the fire of pride, which is his *servant* and not of the flame which, bursting forth, defies all his efforts at control, becomes itself the master, and consumes all that is highest and noblest in his nature. And as to self-respect, it is only another condition of this same pride, and unlike it in nothing so much, as that we need never fear the possession of too much of it. It is even the nobler quality of the two, holding as it does a perpetual barrier of shame between us and every mean or ignoble action, and creating within us a wholesome love for all that is generous and excellent in life. Believe me, my friend, in exactly the same proportion that we respect ourselves, do we hold in respect all that is noble and good."

"You grow strangely warm of your theme," said Watterson; "I was only jesting in what I said. Let us step in here," continued he, as we came abreast a restaurant—come; we will have a sociable glass together and you will forget my hasty insinuations."

I consented and followed him in; and here the "glance" must end; for modest eyes should never pierce beyond the screen which shuts off the view of a bar.

Thus then, and in this spirit, did we begin our night of imprudent revelry. * * * * *
At two o'clock in the morning, much worn and jaded, we gained our hotel. A party of six or eight, all wearing the federal blue, were lounging about the ante-room, some preparing for bed, others reading, and a few writing; and as we passed up to the counter for a candle and the key to our bed-room, I caught some fragments of their conversation, which I soon found concerned myself most vitally.

"What did you say the reward was?" asked one.

"Two fifty," replied an officer in undress uniform, as he stretched himself and yawned.

"But how the devil did he escape?" asked another.

"Walked leisurely out with some visitors who had a pass," continued the officer; "the fellow is bold enough at any rate."

"And you say old 'Marchbanks' betrayed him, did he?"

"So I learn. It seems the judge had in a moment of generosity given him twenty dollars to aid his escape, but soon regretting it (most likely through respect for his own neck), he determined to out with the whole business."

"And so he peached?"

"Not for two hours or more after the fellow had gone; for one of the latter's friends got wind of the judge's intention, and enticing him into a room on some pretense or other, he locked the door and threw the key out of the window."

"No!" said several in a breath, "and how did the pompous old rascal stand that?"

"Oh," said the officer, "there was nothing for it but to submit, for all he fumed and swore beneath his breath; for Putnam, his captor, is a giant in size and he swore he'd break every bone in the judge's body if he spoke a word above a whisper for two hours by the clock."

A roar of laughter followed this anecdote, in the midst of which Watterson and I made our escape.

* * * . * * * *

Many were the thoughts which crowded upon me as I lay awake that night beside my sleeping companion, and many were the emotions born of them. I was still awake when the clock struck four, but soon thereafter exhausted nature claimed her prerogative and gradually I fell into a deep slumber.

Note to chapter XVIII.—The incident recorded in the latter portion of this chapter, in which "Judge Marchbanks" plays, if not an ignoble at least a doubtful part, was given to the author in all good faith as *fact*. The author however, whose age did not exceed a half dozen years at the time the incident occurred, (if it *did* occur) and who therefore has no personal knowledge concerning it, desires to give to the public so much of it as concerns Judge Marchbanks as "mere rumor."   AUTHOR.

CHAPTER XIX.

A loud knocking awoke me, and rousing myself with a great effort I sung out, "Helloa!"

"Seb ner 'clock, sir," said a voice without.

"Seven o'clock already? and what time does the train leave for Wartrace?"

"Zactly at eight, sir."

"Then we haven't much time. Prepare breakfast for two in fifteen minutes."

"All right, sir."

I awoke Watterson at once, and making a hasty toilet we descended to breakfast. We were not long here, for although the meal was excellent, neither of us could eat. We drank some ice-water with mighty relish and eyed each other askance.

"What is it?" said I.

"Me? oh, nothing," said Watterson.

I sipped my coffee lazily, but it did not suit my taste and I tried another glass of water. Watterson followed my example. He was a thought more nervous than I, however, and he did exactly what it had cost me a tremendous effort myself to avoid—he spilt half his coffee on the cloth. "Curse the luck," he muttered, looking at me strangely, almost pleadingly.

"How now," said I.

"I was thinking," said he.

"And so was I."

"Good," said he, rubbing his palms together eagerly; "not too strong, you know, but long and with a dash of sugar in it."

"Wouldn't seltzer be better than water?"

"I think it would."

We beckoned to the waiter and gave him our order, and while he was gone I indulged in a bit of moralizing.

"A fellow not only spends all of his money in a night of debauch," said I, my heart sinking at the thought of the insignificant balance in my pocket; "but he throws away his appetite along with it."

"And buys himself a nasty headache," said Watterson, clasping his forehead and groaning.

"Never mind," said I with a laugh, "here comes the waiter with the 'hair of the dog.'"

"I need it," said the other, "for I've been badly bitten."

No sooner had we swallowed our liquor than Watterson declared his head was already better, and indeed I felt an instantaneous improvement in my own feelings. By mutual consent we now arose, and leaving our untasted breakfast, hurried to the office. Arriving here we paid our score and bidding farewell to the sleek-headed clerk, took our departure for the train. On our way thither we amused ourselves by admiring and commenting upon the many magnificent dwellings which we passed, and which, despite the presence of war, looked peaceful and tranquil in the calm of the morning. A very tender chord in our hearts was touched as we gazed upon these pictures, every tint and feature of which recalled something of our own deserted homes.

"Look, Watterson, at this," said I, as we came abreast a handsome dwelling shrouded by tall oaks, and a smaller growth of evergreens; "is there not something more than beautiful there? Do you not feel a sense of tranquil happiness steal over you as you look upon such a picture as this?"

"It is a lovely spot," said he, pausing to admire the place; "you perceive that Nature is the gardener here, for, except that trimmed hedge of box which lines the long gravel walk leading to the house, the garden is untouched by the hand of man. There is no trim propriety here, none of that fastidious neatness which smacks of a prude indoors. What a wealth of vegetation, what a tangled mass of leafy beauty. Both beautiful and natural," continued he, musing, "how rare the combination, and yet, in this instance, how exactly in keeping with the mistress."

"Ha," said I, "you know who dwells here, then?"

"Know her? Who does not know Mrs. Nickolson?"

"Mrs. Nickolson!" I exclaimed, "and is this her residence?"

"Ask that driver," said he, pointing toward a carriage which at that moment stopped at the gate.

"It is of no use," said I, "for I know the equipage. And so you know her, Watterson?"

"That do I, man, but let us hasten on, I fear even now we are late."

"Must we go, then; can we not wait to see her as she takes her carriage?"

"We will be too late," said he, looking at his watch. "It is already ten minutes to eight."

Although forced by circumstances to leave the spot, I looked back yearningly towards it at every few paces, and it was not until we had turned a corner, shutting off the view, that I could completely master my hesitation and resign the half-formed idea of turning back. In recalling this hesitancy of manner, and this constant looking behind me, I cannot help thinking how small and apparently insignificant are the events which sometimes shape the entire course of our lives. For instance, had we not paused to admire this beautiful home, and had I not in doing so gained the knowledge of its being Mrs. Nickolson's, or had I, even after acquiring this knowledge, passed on without taking special notice of it, nor marked well the way which led to it, in all human probability I had not lived to chronicle these events. Wherefore, and in what wise will soon appear. We walked briskly for a couple of squares, and turning a corner came full upon the depot.

"Here we are with four minutes to spare," cried Watterson, as we gained the entrance to the depot; "Wait here for me, while I run across the street and get a cigar."

I bought the morning's paper from a newsboy, and leaning against the side of the great building I began to glance at the headings. I had scarcely opened the sheet, however, when I felt a touch upon my arm, and immediately a suppressed voice said in my ear:

"Don't look up from your paper, don't utter a word, but listen. If you board that train you are lost. You must leave this, but not too suddenly. Hist, you must *seem* to transact some business, and do it openly. Draw on your ingenuity, and luck to you. Don't hesitate, do as I say, I am Brown, your room-mate, good-bye."

I did not move a muscle, nor did I once raise my eyes from the paper. The printed words swam before me and my heart beat against my side furiously, but not from fear. I became possessed, rather, of that exultant excitement which accompanies a sense of abundant strength and courage, and as rapidly as the warning was given I found time while listening to it to resolve that I would die sooner than again become a prisoner. In this spirit I folded the paper leisurely, and muttering something about the dearth of news proceeded to elbow my way through the crowd toward the ticket office. By dint of a determined will, materially assisted by a pair of stout shoulders, I soon arrived within six or eight feet of the window, and this being near enough for my purpose, I inquired of the agent in rather a loud voice at what hour the train from Shelbyville would arrive.

"Nine thirty," said he.

"What," said I, with a well feigned gesture of impatience, "they told me it was eight thirty. Confound their stupidity," I continued, in a lower voice, as I began to edge my way out of the crowd, "I suppose there is nothing for it but to make my way back to the hotel."

By this time I had reached a side door, through which I passed, and without pausing to consider what route I should take, I began instinctively to retrace my steps toward the "St. Clouds." I pursued my way leisurely for some moments, and not until I had turned the first corner, and lost completely the view of the depot, did I quicken my pace. A few moments' walk brought me in sight of Mrs. Nickolson's residence, and I saw with much delight that the carriage still stood at the gate. "That means she is still at home," I thought, and without inquiring why, I felt this to be a most fortunate circumstance. Following the same impulse that had guided me up to this moment, I crossed over the street and reached the gate. The driver touched his hat as I essayed to open it.

"This is Mrs. Nickolson's?" I asked.

"Yes, sir."

"And she is at home?"

"Yes, sir."

"Thank you," said I, and without waiting to learn more, I walked boldly through the gate and rapidly up the graveled walk leading to the house.

CHAPTER XX.

Mrs. Nickolson in person met me at the door, and recognizing me at once, she started and turned pale.

"Rash boy," she said, half below her breath, "and is this the only disguise you have worn since your escape?" She passed me hurriedly and closed the front door, then opening another which led into a sitting room, she motioned me to enter. Following me in, she immediately closed the door, and seating herself upon a sofa, beckoned me to sit at her side. I obeyed, and was about to speak, but she raised her hand in token of silence.

"Wait," she said, "let me think," and leaning forward she clasped her forehead in both hands, and with closed eyes, sat motionless and silent for full a moment. I watched her closely during this time with increasing surprise and even alarm, for I perceived that she was greatly excited. Her breath came quickly and her bosom heaved in rapid concert. I was about to express my uneasiness concerning her when, with a sudden and single motion, she sprang to her feet and began to walk rapidly to and fro. Still more alarmed, I arose also and looked hurriedly around me for a bell rope, with the half-formed idea of ringing for a servant; but divining my intention, she approached me, and laying her hand upon my arm, begged that I would resume my seat.

"I am not well to-day," she said, dropping heavily upon the sofa; "I have lost much rest of late, and my nerves are all unstrung. But I am better and stronger now," she continued, as several times she passed her hand rapidly over her forehead, as if to brush away that which distressed her; "and now, tell me of yourself. Where did you spend the night; why are you not miles away; and lastly, why are you *here?*"

"You have heard in what manner I escaped, madam?" I began.

"Yes," she said, "I have heard it all up to the time you were betrayed."

"Ha," I exclaimed, "that story is true then?"

"I can scarcely believe it," said she, thoughtfully, "but after all I have heard, I am forced to do so against my will, but go on, go on."

In as few words as possible, I now acquainted her with all that had befallen me from the time of my escape to the moment of entering her house, and finished by imploring her to tell me frankly whether my presence there had caused the alarm which she evidently felt. "I beseech you to tell me this, madam," I said, "and if it be as I fear, you must allow me to take my immediate departure. I should never forgive myself"—

"No, no," she said, interrupting me, "I am abundantly repaid for any momentary uneasiness your presence may have caused me in knowing that you are still safe; but do you know that a reward has been offered for your apprehension; that the city swarms with patrol who are hunting you down; and worst of all, that Douglass is pursuing you with a vindictiveness, nothing short of demon-like? It is he whom I fear more than all the rest. Such hate as his is far-sighted, unwearying and subtle, and he will hound you to the very ends of the earth if he but find your track. Not twenty minutes ago, he passed this house, and although he scarcely seemed to take special notice of it, yet he did look toward it, and I caught the look in his eye. It was wild, haggard and vengeful, and I could not but think that he suspected me of harboring you. Your coming so soon after this will explain my sudden weakness, but that is past."

In my surprise at this intelligence I was again upon the point of speaking, but she quickly stopped me.

"This is a time for action—not for words," she said, "come with me."

She opened a side door as she spoke and led me into a library.

"Now," she continued, "you must remain here for half an hour. If, while I am away, a lady comes to keep you company, you may trust her implicitly, she is one of the society and will tell you what to do, in case any one else calls. For half an hour, then, good-bye; but stay, are you armed?"

"No, madam." I answered; "unhappily, I am not."

"Then, here," she said, taking a Colt's six-shooter from behind a picture on the mantel and handing it to me; "preserve your life, but remember, *thou shalt do no murder.*"

I kissed the hand which held it, while I possessed myself of the weapon, and as I released it she hurried from the room.

I now began to examine my prize with much pride and interest, and to wonder whether half a dozen of the enemy could capture me while I held it. "A trusty weapon," I muttered, trying the lock and admiring the mechanism; "six chambers, which, if none hang fire, means six lives between me and captivity. Now, indeed, is there a chance for me."

I was still admiring my treasure when the door opened and a lady entered. This was she of whom Mrs. Nickolson had spoken. Her name I have completely forgotten, if, indeed, I ever heard it; but I remember well that she was strikingly handsome and that her manners were most engaging. In her company time flew rapidly, and I had scarcely missed my benefactress ere she returned. She bustled into the room with an armful of bundles, and I perceived at once that she had regained her accustomed buoyancy of spirits.

"You see I am back already," said she, dropping into a seat at my side, "and better still, I have arranged everything. I have seen Roberts, who will be waiting for us in fifteen minutes, and I have here everything you require. Now, first, here are some cartridges for your pistol, and here is a duster (which you can wear over your coat, you know), and this is a hat. I don't like the hat you wear; it is of unusual shape and may excite remark; and this is a piece of chalk. You smile, but I have not told you, you are to play sick. Here, come to this glass and chalk your face well; preserve what is left, for you may need it again. Now, look as sick as ever you can; rumple your hair—it is too smooth by far; a sick man never wears his hair like that. Pull it down on your forehead—so. Now, that expression again—are you sure you can put it on at will? You had better practice it before the glass; *there*, you have it now to perfection. Put on your duster now; let me hold it for you; and the hat; that's it, now come, we must be off."

I was indeed a miserable looking object, as with one

9

of the ladies supporting(?) me on either side, I walked
slowly and laboriously from the house and took my
way toward the waiting carriage. As we reached the
gate I heard the sound of approaching footsteps and
the clanking of sabres, and at the same instant I felt a
sudden pressure upon my arm, which I knew was
meant as a warning. My heart leaped to my throat,
but I did not so much as open my half-closed eyes,
nor did I raise my head, which had fallen listlessly forward upon my chest. There were a few low-spoken
words of salutation, and the gate swung open.

"Whom have we here?" said a strange voice.

"Ah, poor fellow," said Mrs. Nickolson; "pray,
help us lift him into the carriage. He is the son of
an old and dear friend of mine, and has been very ill
for some time. I am taking him to a friend's house,
where he can have better attention than I can possibly
give him."

While she was yet speaking strong arms were
lifting me bodily into the carriage, but to whom they
belonged I did not know. As I gained the seat I fell
heavily upon it, particular in nothing save that my
head should fall in such a position as to effectually
screen my face from view; and thus I lay, groaning,
gasping for breath and performing in pantomime, all
the horrible contortions of a man about to take his
unwilling departure from this world. The ladies followed quickly in, and one of them began to fan me
vigorously while the other felt my pulse.

"I am *so* much obliged, gentlemen," said Mrs.
Nickolson, after cautioning the driver to move
very slowly, and to be careful in avoiding the rocks
and rough places.

"Not at all, madam," said the strange voice again.

"Poor fellow, he seems to be very bad, indeed. I hope he will soon be better. Good morning."

"Thank you, sir; good morning."

The carriage moved slowly off, and I opened my eyes. "Am I better now, ladies?" said I.

"Yes," said Mrs. Nickolson, "I think you are much better now."

I sprang at once into a sitting posture.

"And who were my humane and sympathizing friends, madam?"

"Two friends of mine," said she, quietly; "*both Union officers.*"

"I divined the truth, then," said I, laughing; "and how did I play my part?"

"You are a very prince among actors, sir," said she, herself beginning to laugh, "and if you survive the war, you should go at once upon the stage. But I think we may quicken our pace," continued she, leaning forward and hailing the driver; "Tom! Tom!"

"Yas, Missis."

"You may drive up now; the gentleman is better."

"Fo' de Lord, Missis," said Tom, with difficulty restraining a laugh, "it tek you for fool dem Yankey. De gemmun ain't bin sick frum de fus'; him well es me dis minit."

"You know entirely too much, Tom," said Mrs. Nickolson, frowning with mock severity.

An illy-suppressed guffaw, and a loud crack of the whip followed this rebuke, and despite the clouds of war which rolled dark and ominous on every hand, we rattled along the stony pavements, a merry party.

CHAPTER XXI.

The carriage drew up suddenly on M—— street, but a few doors from the corner of Church.

"Was he there, Tom?" asked Mrs. Nickolson of the driver.

"Yas 'um," said Tom, "right on de corner, mum; I shum, dey look dis way now."

"All right, then, drive up to the sidewalk; and now," she continued, turning to me, "you must leave us here. Walk straight back to Church—a friend awaits you there. Meet him cordially, as you would meet an old friend, and put yourself under his guidance. It is not likely we will meet again, but you will hear of me, if not from me. Good-bye."

"But how am I to know this friend of yours, madam?" I asked.

"Oh, he will know you," said she; "indeed, as you have alighted he sees you already. His name is Tom Roberts, and that is all you need know."

"Then, good-bye, madam. I know not how to thank you for all your generous kindness. Would that my heart could speak it, for my lips cannot. I trust we will meet—"

"Yes, yes," said she hurriedly, "we will meet again, I hope, but we must part now; go at once; good-bye. Ready, Tom."

What a heavy heart was mine as I stood gazing upon the heartless vehicle wheeling away my best, my only friend. Dimly, through gathering tears, I watched it till it turned a distant corner and left me wholly deserted.

With an effort I shook off my sadness and walked
rapidly toward Church street, at the corner of which
stood a young man lazily puffing a cigar. At first he
took no notice of me, and I had begun to fear he was
the wrong person, when looking up of a sudden, he
broke into a broad grin, and moving toward me, extended his hand, and cried:

"Why, Cousin Willie, where did you spring from ?"

Determined not to be outdone, I shook his hand
warmly, and promptly replied :

"From Shelbyville. How lucky I should have met
you."

"Lucky, indeed," said he. "I am on my way to the
Suwanee; will you go along ? Of course you will.
My father (your uncle) keeps the Suwanee House, and
there you will put up. How did you leave them
all ?"

"Quite well," I said. "You say my uncle is well ;
and how is my dear aunt ?"

"Humph; you know she is dead."

A shade of sadness passed over his face as he said
this and his manner changed at once.

"You must know," said he, "that my father is a
Union man ; therefore, you must not see him. I will
take you to a third-story room (he seldom gets up so
high), and there you will have to remain in the character of a sick man for a day or two—perhaps a week.
Meanwhile, the lady you have just left will be working to procure you a pass out of the city. My name
is Thomas—Tom, for short; and yours is Willie. Sur-
names are scarcely necessary and can be manufactured
if occasion requires. Now, here we are at the hotel;
follow me right up."

We mounted to the third story and Roberts ushered
me into a small but neatly-arranged room. Here, af-

ter looking to my comfort in various ways, he left me; and here I was destined to spend three days and nights. These were without incident. My meals came to me regularly, and various books and newspapers made their appearance from time to time. Once I was visited by a young lady who introduced herself as Miss Roberts—Tom's sister. I enjoyed her one visit immensely and made her promise to repeat it, but this she never did, probably because I left before she found a second opportunity. Young Tom I saw each night, but seldom in the day, and from him and the papers with which he kindly supplied me I learned the current news of the period. The war was waging fiercely and some of the events of the day were momentous, but it is not my province to speak of them. As to the search after myself, it had grown less and less vigorous, and was by this time (the third day of my freedom) well nigh abandoned, so far at least as the city was concerned. It was currently reported, however, that a certain officer (name and rank unknown to Roberts,) had on that morning left the city in charge of half a dozen men with the avowed intention of "bringing in the spy." This officer, so said rumor, had affected a knowledge of the whereabouts of the "spy," upon which representation he had been allowed to go upon what most people considered "a wild goose chase." I paid little attention to this story, treating it rather as favorable to my final escape than otherwise.

"And what of Mrs. Nickolson?" I asked of Roberts, who had just related the above.

"I saw her an hour ago," said he, "and she bade me tell you not to despair, and that you might hope to hear from her to-morrow. It has been rather difficult, I fancy, to procure you a pass through the lines at

this moment, even before the noise of your escape
has died away; but if any one can do it Mrs. Nickolson can, so never fear. I rather think from the manner in which she spoke this morning that she has
already hit upon a plan which she will reveal to us
before many hours."

Soon after this Roberts left me. His predictions
were destined to be fulfilled. On the next day he
came to me at noon.

"What did I tell you?" said he, handing me a note,
"read that, or better still, I will read it to you; listen:

'AT HOME—12 o'clock.

'Dear Tom—(you see she calls me Tom) I have
met with a deplorable loss.' (Ha, ha, ha.)

"What are you laughing at?" said I; "who is the
note from?"

"Oh, you will soon see," said he, "only listen. 'I
have met with a deplorable loss in the sudden death
(ha, ha, ha,) of one of my carriage horses and I want
you to help in procuring another. Poor 'Bunkum,'
(that's the horse,) poor 'Bunkum' was taken suddenly
sick last night, and despite every effort to save him he
died at daylight this morning. Now I know of but one
other horse that will match 'Progress,' (that's the other)
and he is at Lebanon. But how am I to get him? I have
just been to the Provost-marshal's on foot, (ha, ha,) and
he has kindly given me a pass for our friend 'Mr. W.
W. Wyatt.' I mentioned Mr. Wyatt to the Provost
because I knew he was trustworthy, and I feel sure
that under the circumstances *he could be persuaded to
go.* (That part is underscored, he, he, he.) Having
done so much, can you do the rest for me? that is,
can you find Mr. Wyatt and arrange with him to
leave by the eight o'clock stage in the morning? I

have already written to Lebanon, and the horse will be ready for him upon his arrival. Let him ask for Mr. King, the livery stable man, and introduce himself. Tell me to-morrow if you have accomplished this, and very much oblige

     'Truly Yours,   Mrs. Nickolson.

'P. S.—I enclose the pass.'

"Which she *has* done, by the Lord, for here it is. Now, sir, what do you make of *that ?*"

"Oh, it is plain enough," I answered, "of course *I* am W. W. Wyatt."

"Certainly, and you leave us in the morning; but what think you of the horse story ? Ha, ha, ha."

I joined in his laugh, but my mirth was scarcely sincere, for another sentiment filled my heart at the moment.

CHAPTER XXII.

Mrs. Nickolson was mistaken as to the hour at which the coach departed for Lebanon, and although I was quite ready for the road by seven o'clock, I awaited with burning impatience until half past three in the afternoon before that lumbering equipage was announced. Never before was porter's voice as welcome as that which cried, "All aboard for Lebanon," and almost before its harsh echoes had died away I stood ready at the door, passport in hand.

"All right, Mr. Wyatt; step in, sir," said the guard, returning me my pass, and I did not wait for a second invitation. The door slammed upon me and we rattled away.

I was rather pleased to find that I was the only occupant of the coach, and was proportionately disappointed when we stopped before a crazy-looking residence on the outskirts of the city. Here an old lady shawled, bonneted and gloved, and a young man, evidently her son and the apple of her eye, got in. They kept aloof from me, however, talking incessantly upon family matters, and I soon forgot their presence and gave myself wholly up to the enjoyment of that freedom of which I had so long been deprived. Ah, my kind-hearted reader, believe me, there are few experiences half so delightful in this life as the sweet consciousness of freedom after a long captivity. How fervently and sincerely I now blessed Mrs. Nickolson and the others who had befriended me, and how I longed to leave the sluggish coach, too lazy by half for spirits such as mine, and race and caper at will over the peaceful country through which we were passing. Not content with the mere knowledge of freedom, I burned by actual test to prove and enjoy it. The pure country air was never so sweet as now, the sunshine was never so bright. There was a new beauty in every familiar object that greeted my eyes, and the monotonous character of the scenery never wearied. I had no thought for danger, never once remembering that the sentence of death hung over me. I had no future plans, no present cares, not a thought for anything but the ecstasy of the moment. At any other season, the journey might have been dreary enough, for although we were now some miles from Nashville, scarce a tree had thus far thrown its shadow across our way. Wide expanses of open fields (now neglected and weed-grown) stretched away on either side, presenting a prospect which to less delighted eyes might have appeared decidedly dismal.

It was a hot day, too, "dreadfully, terribly hot," so said my traveling companions; but what cared I for the heat since its very intensity was another evidence of my newly found liberty. "Old Sol seldom finds his way through the bars of a cell," I muttered, and I welcomed his fiercest rays.

During the third hour of our journey we entered a forest of tall beech and pines, with here and there a venerable oak gray with moss and age, and here again I found a new attraction in all that met my eye. Birds of gay plumage, and strange yet once familiar note, hopped from branch to branch of the forest trees which bordered and overhung the road. The gray squirrel, covering his body with his bushy tail, peeped timidly at us from behind a limb, or with one graceful leap reached the ground and scampered away. And the long-eared rabbit, seated on the grassy roadside, took to flight at first sight of us, giving us only a glimpse of his "cotton tail," as with a single bound he disappeared. All this pleased me well—my, my, how well. I never weary thinking of it; I would never tire telling of it. Nay, so pleasant is its recollection that I could dwell upon each little incident of that delightful journey with a fond prolixity, little pleasing to you, most benevolent reader, but fear not. One word more, but a thought, I should say, and I am done. It is this: that among the many and various pleasures of this life, those which defile us not are doubly, trebly dear to us, since they alone are remembered with pleasure. How often in our old age does it happen that our hearts are warmed and softened by the bare remembrance of a single hour of innocent, healthful enjoyment. The cares of a long life vanish as we recite such memories to our children; our age-dimmed eyes sparkle again with the light of youth and happy smiles smooth away the wrinkles, while in the telling we delight both the little ones and ourselves. And what shall be said of those other fleeting pleasures, purchased with our substance, alloyed with wickedness, ofttimes tinctured with actual crime? These we remember (if we allow our thoughts to dwell upon them at all,) only with shame and humiliation. Throughout our age, be it never so repentant, they stand ever ready like clouds o'er the rising sun, to darken and to sully the recollections of our youth.

* * * * * * * *

Darkness soon fell upon us, a cruel inexorable darkness, which deprived me of the scenes I had so long enjoyed. As we seldom think long of what we cannot see (unless the object be very dear indeed to us), I soon forgot that which had entertained me during the day, and began now to give serious thought to my situation. In a hurried conversation, held with Roberts a few hours before my departure, he had advised me not to enter Lebanon, but to stop at a Mr. John Ashworth's, whose residence the coach would pass *en route.* "Ashworth's is only three miles from Lebanon," Roberts had said, "and is immediately upon the pike." I had half determined to follow this advice before leaving, but I had not thought of it since, and now these questions began to puzzle me. Should I stop at Ashworth's, where I was sure of a welcome and all the assistance he could give me, or should I go on to Lebanon, where nothing but uncertainty awaited me? In the latter course there was some risk; in the former scarcely any. This thought decided me, and I immediately hailed the driver and inquired of him how far we were from Lebanon.

"Little better than four miles," said he.

" And do you know where Mr. John Ashworth
lives ?" I asked.

" Right ahead of us, sir ; less than a mile away."

"Then stop when you get there, please ; Mr. Ashworth is an old friend of mine and I think I will
spend the night with him."

" All right, sir ; we'll be there in ten minutes."

" Ten minutes ! A long enough space to look forward to in times like these," I muttered, as I resumed
my seat.

In less than ten minutes the coach stopped, and I
alighted at Mr. Ashworth's door. The family were
seated upon the piazza ; the bright moonlight showed
me so much, as I turned and walked toward the house.
The effect of my approach was three-fold. Two ladies
retired into the house, a man, the only one to be seen,
came forward to the steps as if preparing to exchange
with me either cunning words or leaden bullets, and
a huge mastiff met me at the gate with a savage
growl.

" Is this Mr. Ashworth's residence ?" I cried.

" Yes, sir," said the gentleman, "and this is Mr.
Ashworth ;—quiet there, 'Tug.'"

" Will you kindly step to the gate, sir ? I have
something to say to you," said I. He hesitated a moment, but at length he came forward.

" Well, sir," said he, when he had approached sufficiently near, " I am ready to hear what you have to
say."

" Are you Mr. John Ashworth ?"

" I am, sir."

" Then, in the name of the Confederacy, I claim
your protection. I am an escaped prisoner with a
price upon my head. I am immediately from Nashville; you saw me alight from the stage, and I come
to you directly from Tom Roberts and Mrs. Isaac
Nickolson ; I am working my way to McMinnville,
and—"

"Say no more, sir," said he; "whatever I can do for you shall be done cheerfully. First of all, walk in."

Opening the gate as he spoke he called to his dog and held him by the collar while I entered.

CHAPTER XXIII.

"Walk right up the steps, sir," said Mr. Ashworth, "I must hold this pup until you are indoors, he will not molest you there. I've known the time," he continued, as he slowly followed me toward the house, "when he was the most amiable of dogs, but the all-pervading spirit of war seems to have taken full hold upon him and the very domestics are afraid of him now—walk right up, sir; now, Tug, go and lie down."

"A noble friend and a dangerous enemy, sir," said I.

"He is undoubtedly both," said he, as he mounted the steps; "he is known far and wide, and feared wherever known. I am the only farmer for many a mile around who is safe from the hand of the pilferer, and I would venture to assert he has kept safely for me a hundred times his weight in chickens, eggs, pork and the like. Let me have your hat, sir, and sit here, if you please, until I hang it up; we will exchange confidences on the piazza, if it suits you as well—I will be back in a moment."

He left me for the purpose indicated and had scarcely been gone a moment when the clatter of horses' hoofs fell upon my ear. As I listened the noise increased, and I soon became aware that several horsemen were approaching at a sharp canter. Savage yells and boisterous laughter now and then mingled with the fall of the hoofs, and as my condition demanded extreme caution I called to Mr. Ashworth and asked for his solution of what, in consideration of the state of the country, seemed almost a mystery.

"By the Lord!" said he, after listening for a moment, "they must be Yankees; guerrillas are seldom so noisy, and Confederates never. They are coming from Lebanon straight down the pike, and are evidently drunk. We will let them pass, and it may be prudent for you to step inside until they are gone. It is not likely they will turn up, but if they should you will—ah, here is Mrs. Ashworth; let me introduce 'Mr. What's-name,' my dear; show him into the house until these noisy night-prowlers pass by, and remember whatever happens he must not be seen; now, be quick, they are here already;—and by the Lord," I heard him add as I escaped into the hall, "they are coming up."

Mr. Ashworth was right. The horsemen dashed up to the gate and drew rein at the same moment that the mastiff bounded from the steps to meet them. The hubbub which followed was deafening. All the men began to hail at once; to rattle the gate; to swear at each other, at everything and nothing, while the dog kept up a constant barking by way of protest. They were five in number; this was clearly revealed by the moonlight; and from the manner in which they swayed from side to side in their saddles, I judged that they were all drunk. Further than this I could not discover in the uncertain light.

"Shut up, I say, you (hic) noisy devils," shouted the foremost, who was mounted upon a powerful horse, and had drawn and raised his sabre threateningly above his companions, "how the h—l am I to hear when any one answers? Peace, I say, you devil's imps. Damn that dog," he continued, when quiet had been partially restored, "You, Ashworth, stop his mouth or I'll—"

The report of a pistol followed, and the noble creature, with a last dying yelp, fell upon his side and was still.

It was now Mr. Ashworth's turn to be heard.

"You have killed my dog, sir," cried he; "you drunken vagabond, how dare you"—

"Shut up, John Ashworth," shouted the leader in return, "or we might treat you as we did your dog. Nice fellow you for harboring (hic) spies. Better be thankful for the roof over your head in these days of confis (hic) cation. Now listen to this. We have an idea who you have in there and we are coming in to search your (hic) house. We met the coach, understand, and"—

I waited to hear no more. "Madam," I said, turning to Mrs. Ashworth, who all this time had stood at my side; "if you will show me the way I will escape through the back gate. Fortunately for me these fellows are drunk and have not thought of guarding every approach to the house."

"I am sorry to say you are mistaken, sir." said Miss Ashworth, who had approached and caught my last words, "I have just looked out and there are two men at the back."

"Ha," said I, "then can you secrete me indoors?"

"That will never do," said Miss Ashworth again, "for if they enter, which they seem bent on doing, there is no hiding place here which they may not discover. Mother, you are generally cool in these emergencies; can you not think of something now? Father tells me there is a price upon his head and"—

"A moment," said Mrs. Ashworth, "are you cleanly shaven, sir?"

"Yes, madam," said I, "I was shaved only this morning."

"Then follow me; come, Kate, I shall need your assistance."

The ladies led me quickly upstairs and into a bedroom, and in the twinkling of an eye I was transformed into an aged female, with my hair in a net, my hands in mittens and my face chalked to the whiteness of a sheet."

"Now," said Mrs. Ashworth as she led me to a rocker, which was placed at one corner of the fireplace, "sit here, and we will, if necessary, call you my invalid mother; draw in your feet and let this shawl conceal your hands and as much of your face as is consistent with prudence. Kate, you will sit by him, my daughter, and if those men enter here you must pretend that the noise downstairs has frightened and made ill your old grandmother. I trust this device will keep you safe, sir," said she, turning to me; "I will now leave you and try to acquaint my husband with the scheme. Hark! they are below already."

She left us hurriedly as she concluded, and reaching the entry she leaned over the balustrade and cried:

"Mr. Ashworth, Mr. Ashworth, will you tell those brutal men that they have frightened my poor old mother almost to death. Can they not pursue their search with less noise and fewer curses?"

"They have heard you, my dear," cried Mr. Ashworth from below, "and I hope that for the honor of their flag they will be less boisterous."

"We won't hurt the old 'un," shouted the leader, "my men are outside guarding the doors and (hic) windows, and if your darned scheming husband will only lead the way with the light"—

Here the sound of breaking crockery, followed by Mr. Ashworth's voice in angry protestation, drowned the ruffian's further speech.

Mrs. Ashworth now returned to the room, and as if to prepare her daughter for the coming ordeal, she approached her and took her hand. "Kate," she said, "you will be brave, will you not?"

"Yes, mother," said the young lady as the two embraced, "I am only concerned about—my grandmother there."

" The old grandmother is quite comfortable, I assure you, ladies," said I, "I am only sorry my coming should have"—

" Hist," said Mrs. Ashworth, "to your place by his side, Kate; they are coming upstairs."

We were now given the full benefit of the conversation between Mr. Ashworth and the intruder.

" Hold the light so as I can see." said the latter, "would you have me break my neck down these d—n stairs ?"

" I should not weep my eyes out if you did," returned the host.

" Reckon you wouldn't, but guess I won't (hic) break it just to please you."

" You will have it broken some day whether you will or no, sir," returned the other, "by the Lord I'd do the job for you myself were it not that my wife and child might suffer for it afterward."

" Well," said the man with a laugh, "you are plain spoken, to say the least."

" I generally am, sir."

The door of the room in which we sat was now thrown wide by Mr. Ashworth, who held a lighted lamp in his hand. "This is my daughter's bed-room," I heard him say, "and you cannot enter it. Step up and look in, if you will, but go no further than the door."

"Suppose I say I will," said the other, taking a step forward; but Mr. Ashworth planted himself firmly in the doorway, and raised his arm threateningly. Hitherto I had contented myself with merely listening, but now, fearing that a crisis was at hand, I turned my head sufficiently to behold what was going on. Mrs. Ashworth, fearing for her husband, had risen, however, at the same moment, and was now approaching the door, her figure cutting off my view. It was not, therefore, until she had reached it, and had gently but firmly drawn her husband to one side, that I

10

was enabled to see the intruder, one glance at whom was sufficient to set my blood to boiling, and to fill me with a thousand mad passions, for the drunken wretch before me was none other than "Douglass" himself. I remember little of what transpired within the next few moments. I remember that after many threats and much parleying, and finally through the intercession of Mrs. Ashworth, Douglass was allowed to enter the room. I remember that he peered into every hole and corner of it, that he several times addressed himself half insultingly to Miss Ashworth, and that through it all her father raved and fumed, while his wife endeavored unceasingly to quiet him. I remember so much, yet indistinctly, but I recollect best of all the furious struggle between prudence and passion which all the while possessed me. A dozen times during the few seconds that Douglass remained in the room, was I upon the very verge of springing upon him as a tiger upon his prey, but the presence of the gentle girl at my side as often restrained me. This was not the first time that a cruel fate had tied my hands when most I longed to strike, and I now felt as if further forbearance were a thing impossible. Well for me was it that the temptation lasted but a few seconds, for Douglass left the room almost immediately and, relieved of his presence, I soon regained my self-control. I kept my seat, though not without a powerful effort, until his unsuccessful search had ended, and he had left the house. I heard him descend the stairs, swearing in his disappointed rage at every step. I heard him summon his companions around him and issue his orders to them, to "scatter, and search every d—d rat-hole for ten miles around." I heard them gallop away in every direction, and then, and not until then, did I spring to my feet. Miss Ashworth started back from me with a cry of alarm. Following the direction of her horrified gaze, I looked downward and discovered that I held in my hand the pistol which Mrs. Nickolson had given me. What was more, I found it was ready cocked, but in no wise could I recall when I had drawn it.

"Good heavens!" said Miss Ashworth, "*that* was what I heard 'clicking' all through that dreadful time."

"I—I—ask your pardon, ladies," I stammered. "I could tell you, perhaps, that which would excuse this indiscretion, but I cannot tarry now, I must be off. Let me thank you sincerely for my safety; it has been preserved before by others of your sex, and now, good-bye, and heaven keep you from harm."

"But where are you going?" asked Mrs. Ashworth, as I was bounding from the room; "Good heavens, must you take with you my wrapper, my mittens and my net?"

I halted abruptly, and returned somewhat crestfallen, scarcely liking the laugh which my ridiculous oversight occasioned, and with the assistance of the ladies I soon discarded my borrowed disguise. "Goodbye," I said once more, and this time I descended the stairs. Mr. Ashworth met me as I gained the doorway, but I did not stop to answer his look of inquiry. "I must not delay a moment," I cried, as I rushed past him; "you may think me a madman if you will, but I've no time for explanations now."

Reaching the gate, I passed quickly through it, and a moment later I stood upon the pike.

CHAPTER XXIV.

I paused to listen, but not a sound broke the stillness of the night. The silence somewhat discouraged
me, but resolve such as mine was not to be easily
shaken, and I had soon determined upon a course of
action. "If I cannot hear you, 'Douglass,' at least I
can track you," I muttered, "and if my vengeance be
not so swift as I could wish it, it shall be none the
less complete at the last." I fell upon my hands and
knees and examined the tracks upon the pike. To
my impatient eyes there seemed a million on every
hand, for so beaten by hoofs was the surface that not
one perfect track could I find. "This will never do,"
said I, "woodcraft like mine, could never read *this*
puzzle." I arose and crossed into the adjacent field,
and here again I stopped and examined the ground.
There were tracks wherever I looked, though fewer
than upon the pike, but I could not find among them
the particular impression for which I was searching.
"These are all fresh," I thought, "and they must have
been made by his men, but *he* was not among them."
What to do next I could not determine, and I had
abandoned my search for a moment in order to reflect
upon my situation when a distant whoop fell faintly
upon my ear. It must have been fully a mile away;
nevertheless, I at once determined to proceed in the
direction of the sound. "If I come upon one of his
men," I thought, "I have only to keep sight of him
to finally come upon the master," and this thought
spurring me on I quickened my pace into a run. I
shall never forget that mad midnight chase. Twice
I fell flat, and once I barely escaped falling into a
ditch of water, but nothing checked my headlong

course. I stopped every few moments to listen for a repetition of the whoop, but I heard nothing upon either of these occasions but my own heavy breathing, and the loud beating of my heart. A moment or less spent thus and I would dash onward again, until at length I had crossed the open field and come full upon a dense wood. The blackness of the forest and the thick undergrowth checked me, and I determined after a moment's thought, to sit down and rest, with the hope that something might occur meanwhile, to determine my next step. Upon this resolve I immediately acted, selecting as a seat the butt of a fallen log which I found conveniently near. As I sat thus, out of breath and trembling from exhaustion, I leaned forward and clasped with my hands my burning forehead, and to my horror I discovered that I was hatless. This discovery, together with the fact of my bruised shins, my mud-bespattered clothing and my much-exhausted condition, did much toward bringing me to my senses; for, the more I pondered upon my situation the more convinced I became that I had been upon the very verge of madness. "What, in heaven's name, could I have been thinking of," I muttered; "or have I been thinking at all? Afoot, but poorly armed, and against such odds! Say that I fought them from cover, even then could I expect to hold my own against seven? It is true that I have my pistol but if I killed or disabled one at each fire, there would still be another left; and here am I, bare-headed, bruised and well nigh *hors de combat* before the fight begins. Surely I *must* have been mad." Full of impatience and not a little vexed at myself I sprang to my feet and began to walk to and fro. "Now I wonder," continued I in thought, "if a greater fool than I ever lived. What the deuce am I to do *now?* Ashworth's must be all of a mile away and yet I must return to his place for my hat; oh, stupid, stupid! and where the devil *is* Ashworth's?" I stood still and looked away over the moonlit scene hoping to discover some familiar object which might guide me in retracing my steps, but I could make out nothing but the wide expanse of open field and the dark, wooded background beyond it. "Every portion of the field is as similar as a sheet of water," I muttered again as I continued to scan its surface, "but how now," I suddenly cried, "what is that over yonder?" It was a moving object which had attracted my attention. At first I took it for a cow, or some other animal, but as I continued to look it gradually assumed the shape of a man. My first thought was to conceal myself and await his approach, for he was evidently coming in my direction, but there was a peculiarity about the figure which caused me to stand still and scrutinize it more closely.

" Now, what in the name of all that's peculiar can that fellow be about?" I again soliloquized; " he walks as if his back were broken, and he stumbles from side to side as if he were drunk. One of Douglass' men, of course, but where is his horse? Ah, by heaven, I have it, *he is on my trail.*" I sprang behind the log as I became convinced of this fact, and concealing myself from view I drew forth my revolver and awaited the issue. " Now may fortune grant," I muttered, as my passion began to rise again, " that this may prove to be Douglass himself; the time and the place are both well fitted for the last act of all."

The figure came quickly on, stopping at every dozen paces to rise to its full height and look intently on every hand, then bending low again it approached me swiftly and noiselessly. At length it reached the edge of the timber, and here, as I had done, it paused, seemingly at a loss to determine what next to do. The distance now dividing us was scarcely more than a dozen yards, and as the man straightened himself once more, I began from my ambush to scrutinize his appearance.

" It is not Douglass," I thought, " for he is not in

uniform, nor can it be one of his men for the same reason." This discovery surprised me not a little, and caused me to redouble my scrutiny; but further than that the man was above six feet in height and that he was heavily bearded I could not make out in the uncertain light. I had just made up my mind that if he proved an enemy I must have the drop on him, when he stooped once more, and taking up my trail followed it to within a few feet of where I lay concealed. Had he stepped across the log, as at first he seemed about to do, he must inevitably have planted his feet directly upon me; but, as fate would have it, he turned half round and seated himself exactly upon the spot where, a few minutes before, I myself had sat. I had now but to stretch forth my hand to reach him, and this I determined to do, but before I could make the first motion, the man, to my utter astonishment, burst forth into a low but hearty fit of laughter.

"Well, well," muttered he, when the paroxysm had exhausted him; "well, well, if this ain't a lark, then I never —" He began to laugh again, and this time he wound it up by giving vent to a low, but long-drawn whoop.

All this time I lay still, scarcely breathing as freely as I would have liked, and wondering as I never wondered before, what manner of man was this. I could not determine upon a course of action. The indignant anger which the first sight of him had occasioned, had gradually disappeared, the man's jollity having completely dispelled it, and I was never less in the humor for fighting than I found myself after listening to his mirth. Nay, the sudden and strange turn which affairs had taken began now to strike me as so extremely ridiculous that I could scarcely restrain a laugh myself.

"Well, well," said the individual again, rising to his feet and stretching himself, "the boy is as mad as—as the devil. Of all the freaks; two falls at the least, and—

wonder he didn't break his neck the last time. I'd give a
pretty to come up with him, if only to listen to his
explanations—explanations, the deuce—explanations,
balderdash !"

As the last word left his lips I sprang to my feet with
an ejaculation of joyful surprise.

"McPherson," I cried, as I bounded toward him with
extended hand, "I might have mistaken your voice,
but after hearing that expression, I can no longer
doubt who stands before me. By all that's fortunate,
man, how came you here ?"

"The devil," said the other, returning the pressure
of my hand with an earnestness which made me
wince, "You almost startled me. I thought you could
not be far away, but I'm blowed if I looked for you as
near by as this. Glad to find you, boy, 'pon my
word, I am. I have mourned you as dead, but here
you are in the flesh, and looking particularly well by
moonlight. Well, well; and how have you been,
my poor fellow ? They tried to hang you, eh ? Yes,
I heard all about it, every word; but sit down and let
us not burn daylight, for we have much to talk about;
here, put on your hat."

Something struck me in the breast as he concluded,
then fell to the ground at my feet. I stooped and
picked it up, and to my surprise I recognized my hat.

"You stopped at Ashworth's, then," said I, as I covered my head, "but what carried you there, and how
did you come by my hat ?"

"That will all be revealed in its turn," said McPherson, "but at present, you must allow me to have my
laugh out—don't bother me now."

I stood before him somewhat abashed as he said
this, and my confusion momentarily increased as he
deliberately seated himself upon the log, laid aside his
long rifle, placed one hand upon each of his knees, and
catching my eye, continued for some seconds to gaze
upon me with an expression so reproachful, and yet so

comical and full of mischief, as to make me feel exceedingly small, and somewhat hysterical.

"My young hero," said he, beginning to breathe hard, "my rattle brained mad-cap —"

The laugh choked his further utterance, and for a considerable time his huge frame shook as if racked with the ague.

"My brave boy," said he again, when the fit had ended, "what a scout you would make. I'll recommend you to Morgan, and tell him of this night's exploit—ha, ha, ha—whoop-ee, what a lark !"

"Oh, pshaw," said I, impatiently, "have done with your nonsense, man ; were *you* never imprudent, foolish, or whatever you like, when as young as I ?"

"Why, yes," said he, "many a time; but I was never stark, raving mad like you but *once*, and *that* was when I tried to hoist myself into an apple-tree by pulling at the top of my boots—ha, ha, ha."

"Oh," said I, snapping my fingers and seating myself beside him, "let us talk of something else. I acknowledge to having been 'stark, raving mad,' as you say, but at present I am enjoying a lucid interval, and I pray you have done—unless," I continued, "you would drive me to the conclusion that the malady is contagious. Come, now, where have you been and what have you been doing ? Begin at the beginning, and let me hear all about it."

"Well," said McPherson, wiping his eyes, "I believe I *have* laughed enough for once, but I have little to tell you. You know I'm always on the go, and yet there is a monotony in my life, after all. Let me see. I left you a prisoner, in front of Chattanooga, and you were astraddle of a Yankee, if I mistake not. Tell me, how did you pull through that scrape? I've never heard."

"I will tell you later on," said I, "but at present you have the floor. Did you reach Chattanooga in safety ?"

"I did—you heard my signal, did you not?"

"That did I, and a more welcome sound never gladdened my heart; for I was tortured with anxiety before it came."

"On my account?" said he.

"On your account, of course."

"Thank you. Well, I swam the river, with my valuables between my teeth and my musket strapped to my back, (an old trick of mine), and I saw Ledbetter at sunrise the next morning. I was entrusted with the answers to my dispatches, and I left the city at noon, this time in a boat. I pressed a horse soon after crossing—"

"You 'pressed' a horse?"

"Yes; I borrowed him, and set out after Morgan. I found the latter in Virginia after a week's steady going. (I had to move slowly on account of the prisoners), and"—

"The prisoners? What prisoners?"

"Three whom I caught napping; and—where was I?"

"But tell me how you took the prisoners."

"Oh! balderdash, not now—and as I said before, I reached the general after a week's march. Well I was with him only two days when he sent me, post haste, to Tennessee. I reached the neighborhood of Nashville on the very day of your trial, for I read an account of it and also of your escape in the next morning's paper. Of course I felt concerned about you and I scouted around the city all that day and night trying to pass the pickets, but all I got for my pains was this." He rolled up the sleeve of his left arm as he spoke, and showed me near the elbow the livid track of a bullet.

"It was a close call," he continued before I could speak, "for it passed between my arm and my body, but the rascal got a closer, I fancy."

"And did not the firing bring down the other pickets upon you?" I asked.

"Two or three," said he, "but I soon slipped them, and by sunrise I was safe enough. I slept in the forest during the greater part of that day, and went to Lebanon after nightfall, where I had business and where I remained until yesterday morning."

"Well, and what brought you back and put you at last upon my trail?" said I.

"Why the Nashville paper, of course, which spoke of a certain sergeant with a half dozen men, who had set out in the direction of Lebanon for the avowed purpose of bringing in the spy dead or alive."

"Ha, and you were on *their* trail when you ran across *mine.*"

"Not exactly, for I was keeping them in sight. I found their camp last night."

"And did you notice who was the officer?"

"No, I did not; but after hearing of your to-night's conduct from farmer Ashworth, I can readily guess that you recognized him as your old enemy Douglass; am I correct?"

"You are," said I, "it is he and none other."

"I thought as much, and now let us have *your* story, for there's an end of mine."

"But you have not told me how you came by my hat," said I.

"Oh, I had forgotten," said he, "it was Miss Kate Ashworth who sent it to you, and she bade me say that she hoped her grandmother had not caught a cold for need of it."

"Quite thoughtful in her," said I.

"And quite mischievous, you would add," said the other; "but come, young man," continued he, glancing at the moon which now hung low in the west; "you must begin your narrative, for I will not budge an inch until I hear it, and I fancy there's work ahead of us between this and high noon to-morrow."

"I think I catch your meaning," said I, "and what

you hint at is so much to my liking that I will lose no time in hems and haws."

"All right," said he, "you will find me a good listener. As I have said, I left you astraddle of a Yankee and I find you astraddle of a log. You must fill the gap between them, and then we will to business."

CHAPTER XXV.

The moon had completely disappeared when, as expressed by McPherson, I had "filled the gap" between the Yankee and the log. My companion proved an excellent listener. As I proceeded I was astonished to note with what extreme quickness of perception he comprehended every little detail of my narrative, which, if I attempted to explain, he would wave his hand and say, "Yes, yes, I understand, skip it and go ahead."

Answering my reference to this peculiar gift, McPherson declared that it was the result of the close and constant observation which was one of the first essentials of a scout's existence.

"I have found, after two years of such study," said he, "that the connection between cause and effect is much clearer than is generally believed, and if I am given to know the one I can generally guess pretty correctly at the other. But," continued he, "there is one feature about your mad freak of to-night which I am at a loss to comprehend, for all you call me quick to see. How in the name of all that's wonderful did you hope to pick out from among the hoofmarks of seven horses the peculiar track of the animal ridden by Douglass? Did the beast have a wooden leg, or"--

" Oh," said I, "I noticed upon first seeing the party that the worthy commander's horse was an unusually large one, while those ridden by his men were of the ordinary size."

" And you concluded of course that the largest horse would make the largest track."

" Certainly."

" Well," said the scout, " you may be right and you may be wrong. If your mammoth brute is a common 'hack' the chances are his hoofs *are* the largest, but if he happens to be a blooded animal I'll wager my head his feet are the smallest in the lot. But in view of our surroundings," continued he, " this talk is idle ; I have a proposition to make to you."

" Well, I am listening."

" I told you I had found your friend Douglass's camp."

" Yes."

" Would you like to visit it ?"

" Not a whit, since he has left it."

" But he has not ; that is, I think he has returned to it."

" Ha ; and you can guide me there ?"

" Upon one condition."

" And that is"—

" That you put yourself completely and uncondi- tionally under my orders."

" But what do you propose to do when you get there ?"

" Make a prisoner of your pretty sergeant."

" And the others ?"

" Oh, we'll fight them as long as they fight us, and let them alone after."

" Agreed," I cried, jumping to my feet, "agreed ; but promise me one thing, only one ?"

" I said 'unconditionally.' "

" Yes; but listen before you decide."

" Well."

" Promise that if we succeed in capturing Douglass you will let *me* have the disposal of him."

" Why, what do you suppose I want with him?" said McPherson; " do you think I care for the scoundrel?"

" Then you would simply lend your friendly assistance in forwarding my vengeance?"

" Scarcely that either, boy; for, although I believe in fighting when there's occasion for it, yet I have never sought a quarrel with any one; and as to this thing of vengeance, I have never understood it—can't harbor malice, not I."

" Then why do you propose to guide me to this camp?"

" First, because I would help you to preserve a whole head upon your shoulders, for I see you are bent upon exposing it for these fellows to crack, whether I am with you or no; and secondly, because I have taken a fancy to that noble steed of the sergeant's, and I am determined to test his 'mettle.' "

" Then it *is* your interest in me which actuates you, after all," said I, 'and I appreciate it highly, my kind friend. But tell me, before we set out, what makes you think our birds have returned to the nest."

" They left a jug of whisky there," said McPherson, rising and shouldering his rifle; " and I'll be bound they have returned to finish it. Now let us be off; we have an hour's fast walking ahead of us and if we would beat the daylight we must be moving. Follow me, and remember, no talking and no noise with your feet. If you step in my tracks you will have no occasion to stumble about. Come—forward, march."

McPherson took the lead and for some distance we skirted the edge of the wood, moving in the direction of Nashville. At length my companion stopped and examined, first the ground and then the shrubbery

and some of the trees upon the edge of the forest; but
after some moments spent thus he shook his head
and moved on again, only, however to repeat the process at the distance of perhaps fifty yards further on.
Upon this latter occasion he must have found that for
which he was searching, for after intently scrutinizing
the bark of a tree he beckoned to me to follow him,
and turning abruptly to the right he plunged into
the forest. Here the darkness was so intense and the
undergrowth so densely matted together that our
progress became exceedingly slow and laborious. To
keep together was a thing impossible, so long as we
preserved the silence which McPherson imposed, and
this difficulty at first caused much blundering and
many a halt. At length, however, the scout, with
blunt authority and without a word, grabbed my
right hand and placed within it the butt of his long
rifle, himself seizing the muzzle, and thus linked together we proceeded at a rate of speed which, although
quite slow, was yet by no means consistent with comfort. It was perhaps fortunate that in selecting a
camp Douglass had chosen a spot but a few hundred
yards distant from the field through which we had
just passed; for, had he moved a single rod further
into the forest, I verily believe I never should have
reached his rendezvous. As it was, my patience was
taxed to the utmost limit of its endurance before my
companion halted. I drew a long breath as we paused,
and mentally vowed that my further progress in the
manner described should be limited to not more than
a dozen paces, and I had just sealed the resolve with
an impatient stamp upon the earth when McPherson
stepped backward and directed my attention to a
flickering light faintly discernible in the distance.

"That," said he, "is what we seek; remain here till
I return," and without giving me time either to object or consent to this arrangement, he hurried noiselessly away.

Now, to be alone at night, in a dense and unfamiliar forest, is at no time, and under no circumstances, a situation calculated to produce a soothing effect upon a nervous temperament; but if to the natural perils which surround, or seem to surround, such a situation, be added the presence of a sworn and merciless foe, the position becomes decidedly unenviable. Such, at least, is my individual opinion, based upon the experiences of the night in question. It was less than fear, and more than nervousness, which I felt, and which I am at a loss to describe. I know not, if there be a monosyllabic designation for the intermediate sensation, but if there *is* such a term, it is my opinion that it should be harshly suggestive of everything unpleasant and harrowing to the mind. I squatted down, probably with the idea of occupying less space, and in this position I impatiently awaited the return of the scout. I had remained thus for perhaps fifteen minutes, during which time, to increase my discomfort, a swarm of mosquitoes buzzed around me and stuck their poisonous bills into every exposed square inch of my person, when a low whistle fell upon my ears. This I quickly answered, and soon thereafter McPherson stood at my side.

"Man alive," said I, in a louder tone than suited the scout, "have you been exploring Africa, that you leave me here in torment all this time? What in the devil's name have you been doing?"

"Put a clapper on that tongue of yours," said the other in a whisper, "would you frighten the game, after all this chasing? But why do you prate about 'torment,' who has tormented you?"

"The—ah, mosquitoes," said I, "there's little left of me; but what have you discovered?"

"The camp is there, and every man in it, except the commander himself, is wrapped in a drunken slumber. Their cattle are hitched some fifty yards beyond the rendezvous, and by the way, I've seen the sergeant's horse and examined his hoofs, and I find that they are *not* the largest of the seven. He is a fine-blooded creature, with small keen limbs and feet, and I'm more determined to have him than ever. In fact," he added, with a low chuckle, "I've already saddled and bridled him, and have selected and caparisoned *your* mount also; so now there's nothing left to do but to secure our gay sergeant, and spirit him away while the others sleep. Come, are you ready?"

"Quite ready," said I, "but might it not be prudent to acquaint me with your plans before we start, in order that I may not blunder in my part?"

"It is scarcely necessary," said the other, "but as you desire it, I will tell you the little I have determined upon. First, we will pass the camp, and reaching the horses, we will create a disturbance among them, sufficient to attract the sergeant's attention, and bring him thitherward; then it will be hard lines if we do not find an opportunity to secure the gent, and persuade him to take a ride with us—come along."

"Both simple and plausible," said I, "lead the way."

Five minutes later we had crept sufficiently near to obtain a good view of the encampment, whose wild and picturesque character we could but pause to admire. The spot possessed all the qualities of a secret fastness, being guarded on all sides by a complicated screen of underwood, consisting principally of tall canes, and of those stout and luxuriantly plaited vines, which give so distinct a character to the southern woodland. The group now occupying it consisted of seven men, six of whom, as McPherson had said, were prostrated in a drunken sleep, while the seventh, whom I at once recognized as Douglass, was pacing to and fro, with his hands clasped behind his back and his eyes fixed upon the ground at his feet, as if in deep thought. A small fire of brushwood had been kindled

11

near at hand, whose feeble blaze was just sufficiently strong to throw a ghastly glare over the prostrate "rank and file," and to give to their ungainly forms and ill favored countenances a weird and ghostly appearance. Drinking cups and empty flasks, and here and there disjointed pieces of raw flesh, cleanly polished bones, and "hunks" of bread, lay confusedly scattered about among the forms, while sundry weapons could be seen lying upon the beaten grass, having been carelessly discarded or fallen from the persons of their swaggering masters.

"Those men are as good as dead," whispered McPherson in my ear. "You might fire a cannon over their heads and they would not so much as moan in their sleep; but come, the daylight is upon us."

We moved onward again, silently as before, and a few moments later we had reached the small "clearing" in the forest, in the midst of which the horses of the unconscious enemy stood fastened, their halters having been secured to a long rope, stretched across the opening from one bordering cypress to another. A little behind the animals, and scarcely clear of their heels, were piled their saddles and bridles, together with several saddle-bags and some coils of long rope, the latter to be used for what purpose we could not guess, unless, as McPherson mischievously suggested, they had been prepared especially for my individual benefit. "This shall serve a worthy purpose at any rate," whispered the scout, as he selected one of the coils and proceeded to make a "slip knot" in one end of it; "it shall choke one of the horses until he calls the sergeant to his rescue, and afterward it shall bind the rescuer himself, but before we spring the trap I have a word for you."

" Well," said I, "out with it."

" How do you intend to dispose of your prisoner after we take him ?"

" I have thought of that," said I, "and had determined what to do even before we embarked upon this enterprise. I shall give him the choice of being taken to the nearest confederate post to be there dealt with as a prisoner of war, or of meeting me in single combat. I need not say that I hope he will choose the latter alternative, for I have a heavy account to settle with him."

"Spoken like a soldier," said McPherson, "give the dog a chance for his life, and now we will to business. Do you take the two horses which I've saddled, and with another lead them a little distance into the bush; I will do the rest."

"One other word," said I, "what will we do with the rank and file?"

"Leave them where they are; I havn't the time to bother myself with them, even if I chose to, which I do not."

"Very well," said I. "and now that all is understood, I leave you, to play my part."

Selecting the two equipped horses, with another, which was "barebacked," I led the trio a few paces into the swamp and scarcely had I halted when a commotion among the remaining animals informed me that the scout was already busy in their midst. Turning my attention to the camp, I listened attentively to note the effect of the melee which was momentarily becoming louder; but after listening for some moments and hearing nothing, I began to fear that the irate sergeant had himself fallen asleep among his comrades. This idea began to gain strength and soon took the shape of actual belief, as the moments flew by and there still came no sound from the camp; and I was upon the point of returning to my companion with the half formed idea of proposing that we should "beard the lion in his den," when the commotion suddenly ceased, and the low, but clear and firm challenge of the scout rang out upon the night:

"Hold for your life," it said, "a single word, a motion, and you die in your tracks."

A savage oath quickly followed, immediately succeeded by a blow, and the sound of a falling body, and all was still.

I listened breathlessly for the next sound. That McPherson and Douglass had come to blows I did not doubt, and that the contest had been decided at the first passage seemed equally certain, but which of the two had fallen was a matter of painful doubt which I was impatiently anxious to set at rest. I did not for a moment question the scout's ability to conquer the sergeant in any sort of open contest, but in the darkness, I mentally argued, a treacherous foe such as Douglass might find the opportunity to strike unseen. Scarcely had this fearful possibility flashed through my mind, however, when the sound of cautiously approaching footsteps arrested my attention, and a moment later McPherson stood beside me, having, to my unbounded astonishment, the limp body of the captive sergeant thrown across his shoulders. My surprise was too great to be expressed in words, and I watched the scout in silent wonder as he lightly deposited the body upon the animal prepared for its reception and began to tie it in position.

"There's an impertinent feature about this proceeding," said he when his task was nearly completed, "which tickles me, by the Lord it does. To tie up an officer like that upon his own horse and with his own rope, after knocking him down, haw—haw, haw."

"Have you killed him, McPherson?" I asked.

"Well, it was not my intention to do so," said he, "though I *did* give him a square shoulder lick behind the ear. He is as good as a dead man for the present, however, if not for good; and now bring up the rear; I will lead the sergeant's horse."

McPherson sprang into the saddle as he spoke, and in the order indicated we started in the direction from which we had come.

CHAPTER XXVI.

We passed the sleeping camp in a "dog trot," with no fear of awaking the intoxicated slumberers. The fire had died away, leaving only a few fast decaying embers to mark the spot where it had blazed, but the light of day, which was now fast penetrating the recesses of the forest, had already grown sufficiently strong to reveal the silent figures stretched upon the sward. Notwithstanding the fatigues of the night and the loss of rest, the crisp and bracing air of the morning invigorated me greatly, and as we journeyed along I felt my spirits rising with each onward bound of the spirited animal I bestrode. The feathered inhabitants of the forest began to waken on every hand and to carol forth their gladsome notes in welcome to the coming day. The distant yelp of the wild turkey, as he flew from his roost, recalled the quiet, happy days of the chase, and the mellow notes of the industrious whippoorwill added to the peaceful suggestion. Now and again the loud hooting of an owl startled the air, but only to increase, when its discordant echoes had died away, the sweetness of the softer music which issued from a thousand tiny threats. And not the least enchanting among the many lulling melodies which filled the forest, was the tinkling of a distant cow-bell, whose old, familiar music awakened within me many a treasured memory of home, and filled me with reflections entirely foreign to the stern business before me. Our procession was melancholy enough, heaven knows. The unconscious body at my side might of itself have kept before me the unpleasant realities of the moment, but I thought not of these.

In the presence of so much that was calming and peace-inspiring there was little room for tumult or passion in my soul, and I marked nothing but the gladness which shone forth from every object I beheld. Yea, literally from every object; for the very leaves of the trees, stirred by the gentle breeze, and sparkling each with its separate gem of dew, seemed laughing and dancing in the very ecstasy of delight. And as we approached the open field—memorable from the events of the night—the wind, as if to scatter wide the bounties of heaven, wafted to our grateful nostrils the delightful fragrance of many a woodland flower.

A feeble groan from the prisoner, and an attempt on his part to assume an upright position, rudely awakened me to the less agreeable facts of the present, and spurring forward I reached McPherson's side at the same moment that we emerged into the open pasture.

"We had best stop here," said I, "the light is now sufficient for our purpose, and I would have this unpleasant business at an end. Have you pistols?"

"I have one," said McPherson; "but how do you know he will consent to fight?"

"I will compel him—"

At this moment I inadvertently touched my horse's flank with the heel of my boot, and, plunging suddenly, the animal regained his footing a little to the left of his former position at the same instant that a loud report rang in my ear, and I felt a stinging sensation upon my right cheek. A second report quickly followed, and looking behind me I was just in time to see Douglass throw up his hands and clutch at his horse's mane, while McPherson was vainly endeavoring to gain control over his affrighted and wildly plunging steed.

My attention being momentarily directed toward the latter, I did not notice the wounded man's preparation for his second and last vengeful act, and I started anew as a third pistol shot deafened me. I looked quickly toward Douglass, whose eyes met mine in one swift and terrible glance, as he fell forward upon his horse's neck. That ireful look, which seemed to freeze my very blood, I shall never forget. The smoking revolver fell from his nerveless hand at the same moment that his horse reared and plunged, and dashed madly away. The body swung beneath his belly, entangling his feet and causing him to trip and stumble at every bound, and finally, when a little distance had been compassed, to fall prone upon the earth. Horrified, yet fascinated, we watched to see him rise again, but he did not, and anon we slowly approached the spot, to shudder and grow sick when we had reached it, and to turn our backs upon it and shudder again.

"How did it happen," said I, "for I know very little about it?"

"He must have been armed," said McPherson, "without my knowing it, and at the first opportunity after recovering his senses he used his weapon. I quickly answered his shot and must have hit him hard, for his second attempt to take your life failed for want of strength. The ball he intended for you pierced his horse's head; look and you will see it. Yes," continued he, after a moment's thoughtful pause, "his arm refused to do murder as its last act before it stiffened in death, and—but come, let us go, let us go."

"And leave him there?"

"In the first place. we have no implements with which to bury him, even if we had the time; and—he is so mangled."

"Shall we ride to Ashworth's and request him to have it done ?"

McPherson nodded. "Anything to get away from this," said he, "for I confess I like not the vicinity."

"Come then, I am ready."

We conversed but little now as we rode along, for our thoughts were not of the pleasantest, and we had no mind to exchange them. Having reached a small hillock not far distant, we paused and looked behind us. The sun had just risen, gilding the tips of the forest trees, with his beauteous rays, and the wind had lulled into the gentlest of zephyrs. A tiny cloud of white smoke hung over the spot where the firing had been done; but, other than this, no token remained of the late painful occurrence. The birds sang as sweetly as before, the cow-bell tinkled as peacefully, and nature smiled to the full as complacently. The death of Douglass affected me strangely. For some hours before, and even up to the very moment of its occurrence, it had been the fixed purpose and active business of my life to slay him; yet, now that the deed was done, I could in no wise content myself with the dreadful issue. It was not his death itself that I minded so much as its terrible character; not the end so much as the means employed to attain it. That the man was richly deserving of his fate I could not doubt, but the thought did not dispel the unequal seeming of the contest; and more than all, it detracted not one whit from the revolting memory of his mangled corpse.

Filled with these unpleasant reflections, I turned to McPherson, whose moody silence assured me that his thoughts were in sympathy with my own, and remarked upon the disagreeable termination of what promised to be a very satisfactory enterprise.

"Is not the result precisely what you wished for ?" said he, with a feeble smile.

"The result itself, yes; but"—

"But you would have preferred a more decent and orderly proceeding. Well, so would I, but there is no use to cry over spilt milk, so let us forget it. I could wish, however," he continued, "that I had—that I had searched him—that is all "

"I wish you had," said I, "and I wish also, that I could have spoken to him before it was too late. I should have questioned him concerning this bitter enmity which he bore me, and in which some woman is mysteriously concerned. I have never wronged the man ; I never crossed him, save on that one occasion on the day of my capture; and yet has he pursued me like a blood-hound, from that very hour until this. That there existed some more powerful motive than I am able to assign for hatred such as his, I have never doubted, even before the confirmatory insinuations which he uttered a few days since, and I should like well to have had this hidden motive revealed, but now"—

"It is likely to remain a mystery," broke in McPherson, and before the sentence had left his lips, to my surprise, he threw forward his long rifle and fired on the instant. Looking in the direction of his shot, I was just in time to see a horseman wheel quickly and spur into the thicket from which he had just emerged.

"The distance was too great," said the scout, smiling and proceeding to recharge his rifle after quieting his horse. "Did you see him ?"

"Yes ; one of those we left at the camp."

"So his uniform would indicate ; so come, we must quickly to cover, for although I should not object to a brush with the drunkards, we are too meagerly armed to meet such odds."

"Agreed," said I; "lead on."

Turning our horses' heads in the direction of the pike, which intersected the field at the distance of perhaps a half a mile to eastward, we were upon the point of proceeding when my attention was attracted by a cloud of dust arising from that highway. Mc-Pherson also perceived it at the same moment with myself, and divining its meaning at once, he gave vent to a protracted and significant whistle.

"Horsemen," he said, "and Yankees, by the Lord; see their blue uniforms."

It was too true.

A second glance, showed us a detachment of the enemy's horse of about twenty strong, leisurely pursuing its way in the direction of Lebanon.

"What is to be done now?" said I.

"A question not easily decided," answered the scout. "Let me see, menaced in the rear and blockaded in front; is that what you make of the situation?"

"Yes; but there is no time for parley, man; see, they have already discovered us and have halted."

"Then there is nothing for it but to crawfish, boy, and what is worse, we·must part company. We will stand a better chance separated, and after all, it is only hastening the inevitable. I go towards Nashville, and you in an exactly opposite direction, towards McMinnville, so give me your hand, and good-bye. Now listen; you are armed?"

"I have a revolver; yes."

"Good; then make with all speed for yonder point of woods. The 'blind' road which you will discover just beyond it leads to within a few miles of your destination; follow it, and good luck attend you. Once more farewell; no time for regrets; be gone."

He wrung my hand as he spoke, and wheeling his horse dashed away. A "worm" fence, capped high with "stake and rider," stretched across the field directly ahead of him, immediately beyond which was a strip of wooded land, looking like an outstretched arm of the forest, and for this cover it was soon evident that McPherson was making. But, "how would he cross the fence," was a question which immediately occurred to me, and so interested did I become in the subject that I lost sight of my own danger, and stood my ground, watching the flying horseman with momentarily increasing interest. The obstruction could not have been less than six feet in height, and to attempt the leap with an untried horse seemed to me nothing short of madness. A few breathless seconds ensued, in which I caught myself crying out in anxious warning to the daring rider, and the supreme moment arrived. The manly voice rang out in encouragement; the gallant animal rose high in mid-air, and seeming to pause suspended there for one brief second, landed firmly upon his feet on the other side, having bravely cleared the topmost railing.

A shout of admiration arose from the group of Yankees who, like myself, had stood still in breathless expectancy to watch the daring feat; and as the echo of their voices died away, McPherson answered them with a loud and defiant yell, at the same moment wheeling in his saddle and discharging his rifle full in their faces. When the smoke of his fire had died away, he was lost to view in the friendly cover of the wood, and the Yankees were scattering in hasty pursuit.

It is scarcely necessary to say, provided the reader is but half so well acquainted with the character of the scout as I myself am, that this last and apparently foolhardy action had nothing of bravado in it, but was indeed a well considered effort on the part of the scout, to draw the pursuit after him and away from myself—an act, in short, of brave and surpassing generosity. The device succeeded admirably, for in less time than it takes me to tell it, I found myself alone, the entire troop having entered the wood in eager pursuit of "Slippery Frank."

Now was my chance to escape unnoticed, for I had still to fear the six men of Douglass's command, who might at any moment be expected to appear upon the scene, and I did not neglect the opportunity.

Turning my horse's head in the direction of the point of wood indicated by McPherson, I gave him full rein, and he quickly took me across the intervening space. I gained the cover none too soon, however; for, looking back immediately after halting. I beheld a quartette of the "knights of the forest," gallop into the field and draw rein to reconnoitre. An object lying upon the ground not far distant attracted their attention, and riding up to it they dismounted and gathered around it, awe-struck, and stupefied with horror and amazement.

"I am glad they have found it," I. muttered, "for it saves me both the inconvenience and the danger of a ride to Ashworth's," and thus thinking, I rode away. I was not long in finding the by-path or "blind road," as the scout had called it in imitation of the country-folk, and following this I arrived toward nightfall without further incident at my father's door. I must not ask the reader, however indulgently disposed, to share the memories which linger with me of this brief visit to the home of my childhood. To throw myself into the arms of a beloved and loving family, and to dream away a few short hours amid a thousand tender caresses and fond indulgences; to feel myself for the moment out of the reach of danger, and to *rest* in this peaceful haven, as only a tired soldier can rest, was a privilege and a blessing unspeakably great ; and yet, though all these sweets were mine, there was still a void in my heart which they could not fill. There was not a voice which spoke to me in love, but it lacked the cadence I yearned to hear. There was not an object which met my eye, but it seemed to share my grief and reflect it. The empty chair by the fireside, the seat at the table now filled by another, the bunch of keys hanging at another's side, and the ring on my father's withered finger – all these, and whatever else I looked upon, kept constantly before me the mournful

fact of my mother's death. I visited her grave and
wept over it, and when this was done I felt that my
visit must end. Two short days only did I linger there,
and mounting my horse I rode away again, missing
nothing so much in the parting, as my beloved mother's prayers and blessings.

*   *   *   *   *   *

It was not until I had left the village some miles
behind me that the thought of whither I was going
crossed my mind. I had determined no longer to
pursue the mission which had started me from Atlanta, believing it to be altogether useless on account of
the time which had elapsed since setting out upon it;
and although I could now have been but a few miles
from Dr. Eave's home, I did not think of turning out
of my way to find it. Then whither was I going?

Had I known the probable whereabouts of my old
regiment, it is likely that the knowledge would have
determined me to seek it out and re-enlist with my
former comrades, but having no information whatever
upon this head I did not think twice about it.

And again, I might have joined "Forrest," whom I
knew to be in the immediate vicinity of McMinnville, but Forrest was for the moment inactive, and
this fact alone was sufficient to check at once any idea
I might have conceived of casting my lot with his.
No; I had been idle long enough. The active theatre
of war was to northward, in which direction I was
traveling, and among whose tragic scenes alone could
I be content to play out my further part; and feeling
thus I spurred my horse onward. How I found the
wars and what happened to me for the next few
months must not be told. Enough to say that in the
interim I attached myself to no particular corps, being
obligated to none, but that nevertheless, I saw my full
share of active service.

CHAPTER XXVII.

The months flew rapidly by, the war still furiously raged, and "Old Father Time," moving tirelessly onward toward eternity, strided over many a ghastly battle-field as he went.

Scarce a line there was in this, the eighteen hundred and sixty-second chapter of his massive history, but showed a date upon it registered in blood; and scarce a page, but told some awful tale of death and carnage. Scores of sanguinary battles had been fought, and thousands had bit the dust, deluging the land with their blood; but the end was not yet. "The army of the Cumberland" rested upon its arms in the vicinity of Nashville, with its forty thousand faces turned frowningly toward Murfreesboro, where Bragg lay fortified and expectant. This was early in December. Toward the close of the same month Rosecrans moved his legions a day's march nearer to his waiting adversary and prudently halted, and the Rebel General, seeing only the caution in the act, chuckled in his sleeve and again inspected his intrenchments for the hundredth time. A week of preparation ensued—of silent, dogged, ominous preparation, and the bloody three days' battle began.

It must not be my task to attempt a description of this terrible encounter. The fortunes of war had borne me thither, and of so much of it as directly concerned my individual fortunes I am bound to speak, but for the rest, the historian has left me nothing to tell. The movements of each veteran general have been chronicled again and again, and the story of each heroic charge has been as often told, in language exultant with pride and eloquent with enthusiastic praise. Whether clad in the blue or the gray, mortal men never fought more valiantly than upon this bloody field, nor faced the torrents of death with more consummate courage. It is of the third and last day's engagement that I would most particularly speak.

The fury of the first day's fighting had been followed by heavy skirmishing during the next (new year's day, 1863), and the morning of the third day found each army panting from exhaustion and silently preparing for the final crash, which was plainly inevitable. On the two previous days the harvest of death had been terrible. Men had fallen as liberally as the leaves in autumn, and "Hell's Half Acre" had been leveled to the earth, burying beneath its fated timbers hundreds of Sheridan's brave brigade. Whole companies of charging confederates had been blown to atoms at the mouths of the thundering cannon, and now, to bring together their shattered regiments, and prepare them for a final struggle, was a necessity with both armies alike.*

It was during this temporary calm that I found myself anxiously searching among the hospitals in the rear of the confederate army for tidings of my friend McPherson, whom I had just learned was numbered among the "seriously injured." For some time previous to this date I had been on the lookout for the scout, knowing that Morgan, his noble chief, was not far away, but it was not until the day before the struggle began that I found him, and in this wise :

Late in the afternoon of that day, having nothing better to do, I was lounging near a group of officers, among whom was General Bragg in person, when a slight commotion was created in camp by the arrival of a courier, who, mounted upon a powerful horse,

---

*A prominent historian estimates the killed and wounded in this fight at nearly 25,000 men; "of which appalling aggregate about 10,000 were confederates and over 14,000 unionists."

dashed past me and up to the General. I scarcely glanced at the figure as it swept by, for to me the hasty and oft-recurring arrival of a courier was not more significant than might have been a sudden gust of wind proclaiming the approach of a storm, and had I not overheard some remarks made by a couple of passers-by, it is probable that I should have paid no further attention to the event.

"Ye gods, what an animal," said one.

"And how well handled by the dashing dare-devil on his back," said the other; "I'll wager my buttons he is of Morgan's troop."

Very naturally I looked toward the object of this criticism, and at a glance I recognized both horse and rider. I need not say that I was delighted and that I lost no time in meeting the man, whom of all others I most longed to see. Since this meeting and the subsequent half hour which we spent together, I had not seen the scout, and now I was searching for him among the wounded. It was an anxious and painful duty. The hospitals were numerous, and each was full to overflowing. The dead, the wounded, and the dying, lay side by side in never-ending and ghastly array, the cries and groans of the latter falling upon my heart with sickening effect, and moving me to utmost pity. Wherever I looked, some pale and pain-distorted face, seemed imploring me for mercy, or admonishing me to away and avenge the blow which had stamped it with agony, and marked it for death. Cart-load after cart-load of the dead were being hastily taken away for a no less hasty burial, and those that were left (many of them soon to follow) were being hastily, and of a consequence roughly treated by surgeons, who with bared and bloody arms seemed fairly reveling in human gore. But why should I linger over scenes which

I cannot even contemplate without a shudder. * *
* * * Having fruitlessly pursued my search
through as many as a dozen different hospitals, I entered still another, and after a hasty scrutiny of the
recumbent forms which lay nearest around me, I approached a surgeon and describing my friend, asked
if there was such a patient in his ward.

"What was the nature of his wound, sir?" asked
he.

"I have not been able to learn," said I.

"Then I cannot help you. The quickest way is for
you to search for yourself; look around you and —"

A voice from another quarter of the room caught
my ear and I did not wait to hear the last of the surgeon's speech.

"This way, my boy," said the voice, "for I'll wager
my left arm you are looking for me."

A sudden thrill of pleasure shot through me at
sound of i., and I bounded toward the reclining form
of its master even before he had finished his charac-
teristic greeting. While approaching him I noticed
his bloodless face and haggard expression, but what
shocked me most was the sight of the bandaged stump,
and the empty sleeve which hung at his left side.

"My poor fellow," said I; "I have found you at
last, and maimed."

"Yes, and maimed. Better that than this, however," said he, pointing to his head, and smiling faintly; "but were you really searching for me? Yes?
Then I do not owe you my left arm, which, faith,
is forfeit whether I owe it or not, for yonder it lies in
that bundle over there. They took it off an hour ago,
at least so much of it as the shell left me. And how
fares it with you, my lad? Not a scratch, eh?"

12

"No, not a scratch, I am thankful to say, and it almost seems a miracle, for it has been hot out there."

"Hot, indeed; as hot as I have ever seen, and I have had my share of it. But how goes the day? They tell me our army does not fare so well; can this be true?"

"I fear it is. We have been terribly cut to pieces, and although the others have suffered proportionately, yet I cannot but think that 'Old Rosy' has the advantage. At this moment both sides are preparing for the death grapple, which may come within the hour; and when it does come I fear the issue will go against us."

"Give them a cavalry charge," said McPherson, his eyes taking fire at the thought, "a cavalry charge with a man like Morgan to lead it. "That is what they want, and if that infernal Stone river were out of the way it might be done even yet, might it not?"

"My dear friend," said I, "we will leave that to General Bragg, and talk of something else. When were you shot?"

"Late yesterday afternoon. A shell from one of McCook's batteries burst under my horse, killing him and depriving me of my left hand. I managed to scramble from beneath the carcass and make my way to the rear where they stopped the bleeding after I had lost a full gallon, at the least. The rest was done this morning. Yes," continued he, after a pause, "the poor fellow is no more and I owe McCook an everlasting grudge for it."

"Of whom are you speaking?" said I.

"Of Douglass, my horse, whom I named after our famous sergeant, and as good a beast as ever man straddled."

from my breast, like oil poured upon the troubled waters. I speak of my violin."

"Ha! you never told me you were musical, McPherson."

"Musical? Why, man, I was once the chief performer at every country dance for miles around my home. Being too clumsy to enjoy the dance, I always played from choice, and watching the blunders of the careless country folk, I enjoyed myself to the full as much as the veriest jigger among them. Yes, I'm a dear lover of music, and so was my father and all of us, for that matter. My father, did I say? Why, God bless you, the old man worshiped music. 'Frank,' he would say, over and over again, 'the mind is troubled to-night; get down the fiddle, my boy, get down the fiddle'; and I had no need to ask him what to play. It was 'Down Upon the Suwanee River,' or 'Auld Lang Syne,' that he wanted; and I had but to run over the air once or twice when he would lean his head backward upon his chair and close his eyes as if sleeping; and generally," continued the scout, whose voice now trembled with a holy emotion, "generally when I ceased to play, he would jump up suddenly and wipe his spectacles, which he had worn close over his eyes, and before he sat down again he would move his chair nearer to my mother's and fondle her, and make love to her, for the rest —"

His voice died away and he spurred his horse forward with a sudden impulse that left me several lengths behind. I made no effort to regain my place at his side, and it was some time before he drew rein and waited for me to join him. His manner had completely changed when again he spoke.

"What balderdash have I been talking," said he,

"when all this time I am forgetting that I have a message for you."

"From whom—from Jones?"

"Yes; did you get his note?"

"A few words hastily scrawled upon the back of an envelope, saying that he was upon the track of the man who visited the hospital in the morning, and would report later—nothing more."

"He must have written you another, then, which you did not get, for I saw him not more than an hour before you routed me up, and he spoke of having written you what it seems you have not heard."

"And what did he say?"

"That he had traced the unknown visitor to the extent of learning his name and mess, and had visited his tent after the fight with the view of meeting him and arranging an interview with us."

"Well, did he succeed? and what was the man's name?"

"I cannot answer your last question, for if Jones mentioned the name I have forgotten it; and as to the first—the man was killed."

"Killed?"

"Yes, early in this afternoon's engagement."

"Then I am completely baffled, and the past—"

"Has been hidden by the shroud of death," interrupted the scout, "and if you take my advice you will no more seek to pierce its sacred gloom. Where is the use of knowing that which no longer concerns you? There are three freshly dug graves between you and harm; then do not insult the dead by stepping across their ashes, nor disturb their rest by prying into the secrets which are buried with them. Let it alone, boy, let it alone."

"I am inclined to do as you say, McPherson, and

unless the veil of which you spoke is lifted for me, I believe I shall no longer look into the past. Let the secret rest forever."

"So say I; and now I have something more to tell you: I have been furloughed for a month, and I'm going home."

"Ha! and when do you start?"

"In a day or two—a week at furthest. I shall follow Bragg until he pitches his tents again, and after a little preparation I shall set out on horseback. My parents are both dead, but I have a sister and some friends, among whom I can rest until this wound is healed and I learn some tricks with my stump.. What think you of the project?"

"It is the best thing you could do." You are unfit for service now, and exposure such as you must undergo in camp, would only retard the healing of your wound. But I shall hate to lose your companionship, McPherson."

"You cannot accompany me?"

"No; I would like to do so above all things; but I must not."

"Then we must part; for a month at the least."

"At the least," I echoed, and again we rode along in silence.

* * * * * * * *

Most patient reader, my story is told. Its difficult threads; difficult, because hitherto unrecorded and of a consequence half forgotten—have been rescued after twenty years from the slumbering events of the past, and the fabric is before you. Not a dainty fabric, not rich in color, in texture, nor yet in pattern, but woven upon a loom of truth, upon which fact alone is based the hope, that its contemplation may not be considered wholly devoid of interest. My war adventures did not cease with the retreat from Murfreesboro; but during my later experiences, nothing transpired which has to do with the present narrative. I learned no more of Douglass; nothing more of the origin of that all-consuming passion which so ruled his life, and which, with such vindictive persistence, he misdirected against my innocent head. If Douglass mistook me for the soldier who was so exactly my double—as I must believe he did—his error was enormous, almost incredible, yet does every kindred circumstance indicate that this. egregious blunder was actually made. But this is all conjecture; therefore, enough.

* * * * * * * *

McPherson and Dr. Jones both survived the war. The former, happily married and the father of several affectionate children, is to-day a comparatively wealthy farmer, living not far from the capitol city of Georgia; and the latter, at last accounts, was plying his vocation of "M. D." in the city of Nashville, Tennessee.

Mrs. Nickolson still lives. Shortly after my escape from Nashville, she was betrayed by a cowardly renegade, for what object I know not, and was forced to leave the city alone on foot, and in the dead of night, to save herself from imprisonment or worse; but not for long was she friendless, and she made good her escape without encountering any positive suffering. She is well known and well loved, and in many a veteran soldier's home to-day her name is held in uncommon respect, and the little ones lisp it sweetly in their prayers. The people of Nashville know her best.

Dr. Baldwin died toward the close of the war, after a long imprisonment. This good man could at any time have escaped from his weary confinement, whose irksome bitterness did much to hasten his end, by simply signing the oath of allegiance, but he would not.

All honor to his memory, and to his self-forgetting courage. All honor to this humble hero, who preferred a living death, to a life of freedom purchased by the sacrifice of a single principle of right.

Of the other characters herein introduced I will say no more, except it be a word of myself, to be considered as a part of my adieux.

In narrating these personal adventures, I have not sought to screen myself from the lash of public opinion by suppressing or misrepresenting any foolish act of mine, committed in my youth, and which at a maturer age I might myself have condemned. Nor do I to-day, indorse all of the opinions held, the conclusions arrived at and the sentiments fostered by the rash and unreasoning boy, whom I certainly was, twenty odd years ago. Remember this, indulgent reader.

Concerning the mysterious visitations herein described, I have only to say that, trusting alone to memory, I have exaggerated nothing in their connection. The impressions which they made upon me at the time of their happening, and which I have endeavored truthfully to describe, were—be pleased once more to remember—the impressions of a boy, and possibly of a superstitious one besides. As to what my opinion is to-day, I will not venture an expression. For who will rashly argue the mysterious points of contact between the earthly and the spiritual world? Few there are who will even acknowledge to a belief in such a contact; fewer still will argue upon it, and yet, strange inconsistency, how very, very few are those who do not, *to themselves alone,* do homage to the doubt. Let the wise (?) man prate of his philosophy; the soldier boast his valor; the scholar his skepticism, and the worldling laugh his scorn; but with each there comes a time of honest self-confession, when lonely and beset by terrors; the darkness of the forest, the howling of the wind, the rushing of the torrent; these are the moments, and such as these, when instinct smothers argument, and the feeble pigmy man, trembles at his own imaginings.

*　　*　　*　　*　　*　　*

I pause in my task at the sound of a well-known voice addressing me in tones of gentle reproof.

"Come, my husband," it says; "it is past midnight and you should be at rest; lay aside your pen, now; lay aside your pen."

"Yes, dear papa," · chimes in another voice; "pray cease your labors for the night."

"I am coming," I answer; "I am coming at once," and preparing to obey these affectionate admonitions, I bend over these lines for the last time, and only so long as it takes me to write the one word—

"FINIS."